ISBN : 978-1-911424-08-6
SKU/ID: 9781911424086

ORIGINAL COVER:
Title: OUR EDE
Artist: Fabio Perla
Technique: monochrome pencils on card board
Size: 73 x 51 cm
Year: 2016

Editor: Monica Turoni
Book design by: Wolf

Publishing Company:
Black Wolf Edition & Publishing Ltd.
2 Glebe Place, Burntisland KY3 0ES, Scotland
www.blackwolfedition.com

Hazel Stevens

Our EDE

Part One

Hazel Stevens

1 - Ike's Bike

Infuriating and amazing that's the only way to describe my kid sister. At five she would nick my toy cars, strip them down and put them back together again. If I caught her before she got them back in one piece she would look at me, smile and say:

'It'll be okay Am. The pistons were seizing up.'

'What the hell are pistons?' I would demand.

'Dunno,' she would reply and smile sweetly at me.

I was still annoyed by her. We weren't a rich family and my toys meant everything to me, as they would to any nine year old.

When Ede was nine years old she took Mam's prize electric kettle to bits. By there was a rumpus that day. Oh she had put it back together. However, when me Mam came in from shopping and went, as she always did, to make a cuppa, she filled the kettle and water started leaking everywhere. I quickly disappeared. She had left me in charge of Our Ede, so I knew I would be the one who got the blame and there would be hell to pay. I ducked into our back yard, out through the wooden gate and fled down the back alley.

We lived in a nondescript terrace house, rows and rows of them all alike, surrounding the huge weaving mill where me Dad worked. He had clawed his way up to be a foreman, so we were quite well off in the fifties. The war years behind everyone and the country finally looked like it was getting back on its feet.

Mam wanted us to move up in the world and live in one of the new semis they were building on the outskirts of Leeds. Dad always shrugged off this request and reminded Mam firmly.

'I wor born in this house Lib and I'll stay till I go out feet first!'

Mam tried to reason with him, I say reason because I have never heard them argue and I'm in my seventies now and yes although both in their nineties, they still live at number One, Congleton Terrace. The mill closed a long time ago now and it's been made into flats for students, but more of that later. I'm getting side tracked, back to Our Ede, as she was affectionately known.

It seemed the whole family had shortened names. Mam was Lib, short for Elizabeth. My Dad was Alf short for Alfred. My older brother Ike short for Isaac. I was Sam or Am as Our Ede used to call me, short of course, for Samuel. Ede was well, just Ede. I must ask Mam and Dad why they picked that name. It's one of those things you always mean to ask, but never remember to do so.

We all, however, remember that Spring Saturday Ike got his motorbike. It wasn't new or flashy, more like a bike with an engine. We were still agog by it. Our Ede was about ten and just as keen as me to have a go on it. Ike took us on the pillion, very slowly up and down the back alley. Even our Mam had a go. He cursed though when I got mud on it off my shoes. The bike lived under a newly constructed shelter in the back yard, a roof of corrugated iron sheets. When it rained hard in the night, the rattling of the rain on those sheets often kept me awake. Funny how it didn't seem to bother Ike, who shared the back bedroom with me.

Ike adored his motorbike and polished it lovingly every Sunday. I could sense Ede's interest growing in the mechanics of it.

'Keep yer meddlin' fingers off!' Ike warned her ferociously.

Ede was frightened of Ike when he spoke like that. At seventeen he was tall and could frighten me sometimes. I was only three years younger and often wondered when I would grow as tall as Ike. I only came up to his shoulder and still do, come to think of it.

Now remember, I said Our Ede was 'infuriating and amazing'. Well, one Saturday afternoon about a month after Ike's beloved bike arrived. He went off to see the other love of his life — Leeds United try and play football. OK, sorry Leeds United and all fans and even, more so, our Ike. He has followed the ups and downs of this illustrious team since Uncle Fred took him to Elland Road when he was about seven. Ike, I mean, being seven not Uncle Fred! Dad and me are Leeds Rugby supporters, though I don't go as often as Dad does. Ike has no time for rugby, which is a great disappointment to Dad. As we know only too well they have quite a debate about the ethics of rugby versus football.

Anyhow, Ike went off this particular Saturday to Elland Road, with a firm, 'Keep yer sticky mitts off me bike our Ede and you an' all Sam! I will know if either of you so much as laid a finger on it.'

'Yes Ike,' we both mumbled, staring guiltily at his bike as if alarm bells would start ringing. Ede and I were on our own that day. Mum had gone off to see Great Aunt Eliza in Harrogate. Dad was down on the allotment, as Leeds Rugby weren't playing.

I wouldn't have minded going with Dad. I often did, as I loved helping him on the allotment. Weeding, watering and watching stuff grow. When Ede was younger we would both go, not now, she refused point blank. So I had to stay home and 'keep an eye on her'. Oh yes, she still took my toy cars apart and put them back together again and she was always messing with her bike, tightening this, altering that.

'Come on Am,' she cried, even before Ike had probably got no further than the end of the street, 'Let's see what that bike of our Ike's is made of.'

'Oh no! Ede! No! You heard our Ike. I ain't gonna get the wrong side of him. No! No! Do you hear me?' Before she had chance to answer back, I carried on, 'I'm gonna to read. Now you have one of three choices! You either go and call for Lucy, go upstairs, or if you must, sit in the room with me and when I have read me book we'll play a game or something.'

Ede frowned at me and stuck her tongue out, leaping away just in time to dodge my outstretched hand, aimed at giving her a clip round the ear. I couldn't be bothered to chase after her as I usually did. No, let her go and then I would be able to read in peace. I'd borrowed a book on gardening from the library and longed to be able to give Dad a tip or two from it.

'I'm off to Lucy's,' Ede yelled as she slammed the back door. Hearing the back gate slam too I breathed a sigh of relief, settled back in my chair and picked up the book. It wasn't long before I was totally engrossed in how to grow roses.

Little did I know that Ede had opened and slammed shut the back gate without actually going through it. I was oblivious to the outside world for the next hour or two, engrossed in my book. Suddenly the back door flung open with a resounding bang.

'Oh Am!' A small-terrified voice spilled into the room. I leapt to my feet, fear gripping my throat. Our Ede. What had happened? I stared at the trembling figure, her face ashen, her large blue eyes brimming with tears. What on earth had happened to her?

'Ede?' I gasped staring at her, then I saw the oil. She was covered in it, great black hand marks on her dress. I stood and stared, trembling myself now, as the realisation of what she had done spread over me. I feared now not only for her but also for myself and the trouble I would be in for not watching her.

'Ede, no please tell me no, you haven't. Not Ike's bike!' I gabbled at her. 'What the hell have you been doing?!'

'I...I only wanted to...to see what the engine was like.' Huge tears fell down her oil-streaked face as she sobbed her confession.

'No Ede, no, not Ike's bike.' I screamed at her in disbelief.

Ede started to tremble again as she nodded slowly.

'Oh God what have you done!' I pushed past her and stumbled out into the yard. It was littered with nuts and bolts. A slick of oil ran slowly down the yard and under the back gate. The bike had a huge gaping hole where the engine should be. I couldn't believe she had taken the engine out and bits of it lay all over. Ede followed me out, sobbing and sniffing loudly.

'Oh my God Ede, now what? Just get it back together.' I yelled, staring menacingly down at her.

'I...I can't...' She cried, her body shaking as huge great sobs engulfed her.

'What do ya mean you can't?' I paced round her, running my hands through my hair. 'You must.' I yelled, taking her by the shoulders, 'You must!' I felt like throttling her, instead I shook her hard.

'Well I can't!' She wailed, 'I...I don't know what goes where.' She wiped an oily hand over her eyes. I glanced at the kitchen clock. Hell Ike would be back in just over an hour or two at the most, so would me Dad and Mam. What were we going to do? I didn't know the first thing about engines and still don't, I've no interest you see.

'Sid!' I shouted and ran out the back gate, leaving a bemused Ede gawping after me.

I ran down the back alley to my mate Joe's house. He lived at the other end of the terrace and he was just where I knew he would be, in the back yard, polishing his push bike. I almost fell over him as I charged in.

'Sid, where's Sid?' I shouted. Joe was so startled he just pointed to the open back door. I ran inside and found his brother. Sid was sprawled on the sofa, blowing smoke rings into the air.

'Hiya young un,' he said. 'What's up?'

'Ede and our Ike's bike.' I gabbled at him.

Sid was up in a flash and almost shoved me out of their house. He picked up an oily, well-used tool bag from behind the back door, pushed me down the yard and we hurried up the alley together.

'Okay, what's she done now?' Sid smiled as I trotted beside him to keep up with his long loping stride. 'As if I can't guess.'

'Oh Sid, you'll never guess what she's done this afternoon! She er, she's only taken the engine out and can't put it back.'

'Oh bloody hell. It's worse than I thought, if she's done that.'

I turned to look at Sid and could see anxiety all over his face. I knew he would help if he could, but Sid was only a couple of years older than Joe and me. He'd left school and started an apprenticeship with a garage down by the railway. Despite being one of Ike's mates Sid was a bit frightened and in awe of Ike.

'Right Ede, let's see what you have been up to.' Sid said as he pushed open our back gate. Ede was standing in the same place I had left her, staring down at Ike's bike. The sobs had reduced to tears, which she quickly wiped away as she heard Sid's voice.

'What time is Ike 'ome?' Sid asked nervously.

'In about an hour or so,' gulped Ede.

'Right, let's get cracking then. You pass me the tools I ask for Ede, okay?' Sid ordered gently.

Ede nodded and I sat on the back doorstep watching as Sid called for this tool and that tool. Each time our Ede passed them to him without questioning once if she had selected the right one from his tool bag. They worked earnestly for the next forty-five minutes. I kept glancing at the back gate waiting for someone to come through it and all hell break loose. Joe had volunteered to stand guard at the end of the road, the minute he saw any of my family turn into it, he would bike round and warn us.

'Right I think that should do her.' Sid stood up and smiled first at Ede and then at the bike. 'Now this oil and the bike needs cleaning up so I suggest you two get on with that, I'm away home to get a bath before me tea.'

'Thanks Sid,' I sighed in relief, kicking my dumb sister.

'Yeh, ta Sid,' she smiled up at him, adoration spread all over her face. Giving Sid one more sweet sickly smile Ede went into the house.

'OK Sam, get lively and get this lot cleaned up. You'll need bleach I reckon. Hopefully Ike won't know a thing, just tell him you gave it a wash for him. Oh, and by the way, you owe me one.' Sid grinned and left us to it.

Ede reappeared in a clean dress and a bucket of soapy water splashing down the steps. What she would tell Mam about the state of her other dress I didn't want to know.

For the next twenty minutes we scrubbed the yard, washed and polished the bike. Both were shining when Mam came through the back gate, seconds after Joe had arrived to warn us of her approach.

'What on earth!' She exclaimed, as she saw the sparkling white flagstones beneath her feet. 'What have you been doing?' She asked, first looking at me and then Our Ede.

'Oh just cleaning our bikes and Ike's and the yard.' Ede, Joe and I said in unison.

'Good job you have all made too. For all your hard work Joe would you like to stay for tea?' She said knowingly. I knew she thought Joe had inspired us to do the cleaning. I glared at him, envious of her praise. He hadn't done a thing, only rode his bike round to warn us she was coming. Joe smiled sweetly at her. 'No thanks, me Mam's expecting me, gotta go.' He scrambled out of the yard dragging his bike behind him. I knew he didn't want to be here when Ike came home.

'What's he in a rush for?' She asked, staring after Joe.

'Expect his tea is ready.' I shrugged.

'Oh well, good job you two.' She said as she walked into the house, a big smile on her face.

Ede and I stood in silence as she disappeared through the back door.

'Thanks 'Am.' Ede threw her arms round me in a great hug.

'Ger off me will you!' I growled under my breath, 'Next time I am not, I repeat not, bailing you out — got it!' I strode inside, leaving Ede looking somewhat bewildered. I think she thought I was a knight in shining armour — coming to her rescue. No chance! I was saving my own skin. I was still afraid of what Ike would say about his bike being cleaned and if he would know what had happened to it. I fled upstairs.

'I'm off to have a bath.' I yelled to Mam. Well, I daren't go to my room, I shared that with Ike. Best to lock myself in the bathroom out of his way.

I must have dozed off in the bath as the next thing I heard was tapping on the door. It was Ede.

'Go away,' I mumbled sleepily.

'It's OK Am, Ike's home and he's really pleased we made such a good job of cleaning the bike, even though he had warned us not to touch it. It's okay, he's just gone out on it, and it works.' Ede whispered loudly through the door. 'I was mighty scared though 'Am. I have been in my room, told Mam we woz both tired after all that cleaning. I think she thinks we're ill or summat.'

'Shut up Ede and go away.' I didn't want to hear any more.

'Well Mam asked me to come and get you out the bath 'cos Ike's gone for fish and chips. Dad's home too.'

I lay there and closed my eyes again as Our Ede went back downstairs. My nerves couldn't stand an afternoon like this one had been! Next time I vowed, I definitely wouldn't be looking after my brat of a sister ever, ever again! We may have got away with it this time but I couldn't be sure Ike wouldn't hear about it via Sid. I would get out of the bath when I heard Ike come back. As it was we had used quite a lot of hot water scrubbing the yard clean and there was no more left to top up the bath. Eventually I had to get out or freeze to death in the fast cooling water. I'd just have to hope the water heated up again, Ike was bound to be off out tonight and I didn't want a row because I'd used all the hot water.

Ike still wasn't back from the chippy when I went downstairs, Dad was pacing round the kitchen looking at the clock. Mam sat at the table dabbing her eyes.

'Oh Alf you don't think...' Mam's voice trailed off in despair. I looked from one to the other.

'Nay lass,' Dad put a comforting arm round her shoulders. 'Chippy'll be busy that's all, or he's met some lass. You know what our Ike is like.'

'He's been gone over an hour Alf.' Mam stared up at my Dad with the same large blue eyes Our Ede had stared at me with, only a couple of hours earlier.

The realisation of just what Mam and Dad were afraid of hit me like a thunderbolt. What if Ike and the bike had crashed somewhere? What if Sid hadn't got it back together again right and it was his fault? No, it would be Ede's fault. In the living room Ede sat by the fire, staring mournfully into it, she was obviously having exactly the same thoughts as me.

'I'll go and see shall I?' I said, pulling my coat off the back door hook. No one seemed to be listening. I opened the back door and stepped out into the yard, it began to rain and the clean white concrete blotted with huge drops of rain. The back gate came flying open and crashed against the wall making me jump. I looked up to see our Ike pushing his bike through the gate. His face like thunder.

'Ede, Ede. Where are you?!' He screamed.

I retreated hastily back into the house.

Mam pushed past me and ran out into the yard.

'Oh Ike you're okay, you're okay, we thought...' Her voice trailed off as she threw her arms round him. Ike holding the bike with one hand put his free arm around her waist almost lifting her off her feet.

'I'm okay Mam, it's the bike that isn't and I think that might have something to do with my little sister.' Ike's voice dropped menacingly.

'No Ike, they only cleaned your bike and the yard.'

'I think she did more than that Mam.' Ike let her go and put the bike on its stand and strode into the house.

'Sam, Sam what was she doing all afternoon?'

I had backed away into the kitchen. Now unable to move, Ike marched through the door towards me, waiting for an answer. I shrugged and mumbled something incoherent. He brushed me aside and strode into the living room. I followed. Ede sat perfectly still and continued to stare into the fire. How would she get out of this? What would Ike say or do to her and to me? I crept quietly away. OK, I know I'm a coward, but you don't know our Ike! It wasn't as bad as we all feared. Mam leapt across the room, landing in between Ede and Ike, startling them both.

'Oh Ike, thank God you're all right. That damn machine, we were sure you had been in a crash.' Mam spoke quickly, she had tears in her eyes as she clasped both her arms round Ike's towering body. It worked. Ike was like putty in Mam's hands. Ede stood up and backed nervously towards the door, knowing our Mam was giving her time to make herself scarce until Ike had simmered down.

'I'll deal with you later,' Ike snarled. At that Ede fled to the bathroom and in the silence we heard the bolt on the bathroom door being rammed firmly home. This room was the favourite bolt hole of my errant sister and me because you could lock yourself in there, away from the wrath of whoever you had upset, which was usually our Ike. I quickly followed Ede upstairs and went into mine and Ike's bedroom. I prayed he would stay downstairs.

It seemed like an eternity, yet it was under half an hour when Mam shouted up to both of us that tea was ready. The smell of frying bacon had already wafted upstairs and was making my stomach growl with hunger. Ede and I came out from our bolt holes onto the landing at the same time. She smiled at me, her eyes red from crying. I nodded and she followed me downstairs.

Ike sat glowering at us from the other side of the table and we both cautiously sat down. Without a word from any of us we ate our bacon and eggs.

'No more Ede and I mean that!' Ike spoke sharply as he placed his knife and fork side by side on his plate.

'Now Ike what did I say? We are not going to mention anything about it, are we!' Mam told him firmly.

Ike just looked at her and smiled.

Yes, I remember that day like it was yesterday. Sitting at the table my heart beating so loud, I was sure they would all hear it. You might find this strange, but it's perfectly true, the incident with Ike's bike has never ever been mentioned from that day to this. I asked Ede the next day just how terrified was she, I felt sure Ike would not let it rest quite so easily. Ede smiled, shrugged and told me Mam had spoken to her and Ike. She skipped off leaving me even more confused and wary. As I've said before, you don't know our Ike. Perhaps you are getting to know him more now and you can understand why I never mentioned the incident to anyone after that. It seemed as the days went by I had escaped retribution.

Though each time I saw Our Ede gazing longingly at the bike, I reminded her, 'Not on your nelly Ede!'

Whatever had been said to Ede that day for the next few years it had the desired effect. My toy cars were left alone even after I abandoned them. Mum's new kitchen equipment remained untouched. As for Ike's bike although she might gaze longingly at it, I knew she didn't need my warnings. She knew to leave it well and truly alone.

2 - Mrs. Rowntree

I left school the following year and now I was a man, about to make my way in the grown up world. To my great delight I got a job in Warren's plant nursery on the outskirts of Leeds. It meant a half hour bike ride there each morning and another half hour at the end of the day. I didn't mind, it was wonderful leaving behind all the traffic and the streets of endless terrace houses. Going out into the open countryside, the green fields and much fresher air. It was like a dream come true. How I loved those days of bringing on the blooms to sell on Leeds market. Sowing the annual flowering plants and tending to them, very soon became my area and with the latest rock and roll music blaring out of the portable radio from the corner of the huge greenhouse, I worked happily away. Deftly pricking out, potting up and nurturing my babies until they were ready to be dispatched.

A year after I started they decided to open a shop on the nursery site and sell the flowers, plants, plus other garden stuff from there.

I told Mr. Warren he was way behind times. I'd read somewhere a place in Buckinghamshire had been selling plants since the 1700s.

I served in the shop quite often but I didn't like it. I would get all tongue tied and very embarrassed, especially when Mrs Rowntree came in.

Mrs Rowntree was simply gorgeous, I used to tell

my friends she had won bathing beauty competitions and that was how she could afford the big house up near Roundhay Park. I knew she had two full time gardeners. How I envied them working for this vision of loveliness. When it came to buying plants for her garden Mrs Rowntree always came down to the nursery herself. I can picture her now. Okay as she was then I mean! She had long coppery hair, which glinted with flecks of gold when the sun caught it. Her skin was as smooth as silk and her perfectly shaped lips were always covered in red lipstick. This was the only make up she wore I think. Her trim neat figure always smartly clad in a pair slacks teamed with soft pastel jumpers or crisp white blouses, depending on the weather. I guess she must have been about thirty then, which makes her going on ninety now. I wonder if she still wears red lipstick.

Remember I was only just sixteen at the time and all those adolescent hormones we hear about now, must have been raging. I would go back to the greenhouse after serving her, in a dream, imaging what I would do if we were alone. How I would hold her, kiss her, tell her how much I loved her. I knew it could never be, but it still didn't stop me day dreaming.

Life was good, Ike had left home. He'd taken a job down in London, working on the underground railways. They'd found him a flat and everything. He even had a girlfriend, Lily. Poor Lily she must have been at the back end of the queue to Mrs Rowntree when

God was giving out the looks. Her long thin, limp, dirty blonde hair hung like curtains round her equally thin, pinched face. She was just as thin everywhere else and rarely smiled. The few times she came home with Ike she hardly spoke two words to any of us. Ike adored her though and I would often see him giving her the same look he gave his first motorbike.

The bike had been changed and now Ike had a huge one, with gleaming blue and silver bodywork. Our Ede's eyes nearly popped out of her head the first time he came home on it, with Lily clinging onto the pillion, like a limpet. Ike saw the look in Ede's eyes and said very quietly, 'Hands Off!'

Ede nodded but stood for a long while staring at the machine.

The bike nearly filled our tiny back yard. Mam still cursed motor bikes and declared them all to be 'death traps'. She tried and tried to persuade Ike to get a car, but he would have none of it.

Mam also tried and tried to talk to Lily, the first time Ike brought her home, but it was hard going. I sat and listened as Ike babbled on and on about how wonderful London was with it's busy streets, tower blocks and huge shops. I wondered how people survived down there, especially Ike, who lived in North London somewhere. He said it took him over an hour to get out into the countryside and that was on his motor bike! It sounded worse than Leeds and that was bad enough.

In the fifties and sixties, Leeds was spreading at an alarming rate. Around the nurseries, houses were being built as farmers succumbed to the generous packages paid for land by the property developers. Mr Warren, the owner of the nurseries, vowed never to give in to them. He was determined to keep a bit of green and fertile land amongst the plethora of bricks and mortar.

I shuddered at the very thoughts of London and good-humouredly took Ike's ribbing about my work with teeny plants and why hadn't I got a 'bird'. I told him blankly I hadn't time for girls. He then went on about me being queer or summat, whatever that meant. I was very naive in those days. Ike soon shut up about it when Mam came to my defence and told him to leave me alone.

Ike continued to gaze at Lily, his eyes shining. It took mighty strength for me not to shudder again. What did he see in her? She wasn't anywhere close to Mrs. Rowntree who, at that time, was coming every week to buy plants. Why would I want a bird when I had her? Yes, life was good, even if Ike couldn't understand why I didn't want to spread my wings, go to London and be like him. They asked me down to spend the weekend with them. 'A taster.' Ike had said. The very idea of spending time with them being gooey-eyed about each other, in London of all places, no thank you!

On reflection, thinking about those early courtship days of Ike and Lily. I don't think I ever saw her look at Ike in the same gooey-eyed way as he looked at her. She must have though, but I can't recall it. Ike was besotted.

Yes, they even got married a few months later. I

heard Mam say to Dad our Ike would be paying for the wedding. They didn't think this was right. It seemed her folks didn't have any money. Dad grimaced and declared Ike would be paying for the wedding the rest of his life. I wasn't sure then what he meant by that.

Mam, Dad and Ede went down to the wedding. I pleaded work commitments. Well, it was a Saturday, our busiest day. Mr Warren would be only too glad to let me have time off. I couldn't bring myself to. I felt guilty about it, but Ike didn't seem to mind. I knew I wouldn't be missed. Mam would be fussing around like a mother hen.

Ede was so excited and kept prattling on about all the new cars she would see down there. I couldn't think why the cars in London would be any different to the ones up here. But I listened to her childish prattle. Ede was growing up fast. She was very much a tomboy and declined playing with dolls etc. Even her friend Lucy usually had a doll or a soft toy in tow, whenever she came round ours. Not Ede. She had placed all my cast off toy cars in a row on her bedroom window sill.

I digress. More about Ede later. Back to Ike's wedding. A few weeks beforehand, Mam bought Ede a new dress to wear at the wedding.

'It's awful Mam.' Ede wailed, as she appeared in a flouncy array of pink chiffon.

'You look like candy floss.' I said grinning from ear to ear. Remembering the lovely sugary confection we were treated to whenever we went for a day out to Scarborough, in the summer holidays.

We didn't ever go away to stay, Dad liked his home comforts. But we would go for days out on his annual two week holiday, over to the coast or into the Yorkshire Dales.

I deftly dodged Ede's swift hand, and grinned as she tugged the dress this way and that.

'Candy floss.' I repeated, laughing loudly.

'Now Sam, Ede looks, well...lovely.' Mam sighed. 'I think I'll take it in a bit.' She added pulling it together round Ede's back.

'No Mam, it's too tight now,' wailed Ede in abject misery. 'Can't I wear something else? My grey school skirt and white blouse?'

'No. You want to look your best and this is a lovely dress for a wedding' Mam was firm. Ede's face grimaced. She was painfully uncomfortable in the dress. Ede looked more at home in a cut down pair of Dad's dungarees. However, we all knew better than to argue with Mam. Especially when Mam had her mind set on something.

Mam, Dad and Ede would be staying down in London over night and I would be left alone in the house. Dad warned me to keep my mates out. Joe had been badgering me about having a party. To let him bring his mates from the factory. Joe was working there now. How he stuck sweeping floors all day I just don't know. But I knew some of his work-mates and no way would I let a load of yobbos into our house. I tried to tell Dad but I don't think he believed me. I promised and promised there would be no party. Mam finally persuaded

Dad that she trusted me and she knew I would keep my word.

On the wedding day, I was glad I hadn't gone to London. Mrs. Rowntree came in to buy some pot plants for her mother's birthday the next day. She wasn't sure what to get. This was a little unusual. Whenever she bought plants for the garden she would stand in the shop, reel off a list and I would fetch the plants. Not today, I spent a blissful hour walking round the plants in the huge greenhouse with her. We had expanded a lot and now stocked twelve different types of geraniums, or to be correct pelargoniums, plus a variety of others. From house plants with no flowers just leaves or foliage, these were becoming the thing those days, to plants with enormous blooms that almost shouted at you from their pots. She talked easily and asked me lots of questions about the plants which I was glad to be able to answer, I liked to think she was very impressed with my knowledge even though I stammered and blushed a lot. It was like being in a dream and to think I might have missed this to be at Ike's wedding.

Our Ede was full of it of course when they returned. Not so much about the wedding. More about the London transport system. They had even been on the Underground. She ignored my question about how the dress looked.

'I was scared at first Am on the Underground. All you can see out the windows is black walls. But imagine a train that actually goes underground.' Ede seemed totally amazed by it all.

Mam came back wistfully sad and Dad still remonstrated that Ike would be paying for it the rest of his life.

Ike and Lily had their first baby six months later. A boy they called Frankie. Joe asked me if he was named after singer Frankie Vaughan. I told him I doubted this as who would call their kids after singers. I was soon proved wrong when Conway arrived a year later, Shirley and Buddy the twins followed fifteen months after Conway. Our Ike was forced to sell his beloved bike and buy a car then to transport them all about.

We hadn't enough room for them all to stay but they would come for the day every couple of months or so. The house would be filled with screaming kids and smelly nappies. We all sighed with relief as we waved them off in their old Ford Popular car. I swear, each time they visited, Ike looked years older and Lily looked more and more miserable. A lot thinner too, if that were possible, her hair looked greasier and lanker. I felt sure the slightest breeze would knock her over. How she found the strength to lift the chubby, round Frankie and the solid body of Conway at the same time I don't know.

Mam seemed besotted with Shirley. Ike's daughter was so petite and delicate, not a bit like Our Ede had been when she was a baby. I heard Mam comment to Lily how Shirley would look real bonny in pretty dresses. Lily gave a curt nod as she redressed Shirley in Frankie and Conway's hand me down romper suits.

I saw Mam look at Ede when she made this remark. I was surprised to see Mam's eyes fill with sadness.

Our Ede saw her looking and smiled at Mam. Whenever Ede smiled it reached her large, blue eyes and they could light up a whole room. Mam beamed back at her and the look of sadness turned to joy.

As Ede grew older she seemed to grow taller and broader, at almost fourteen she reached my shoulder. I was fast becoming her big, little brother. She was a tomboy through and through, something little Shirley would never be.

Every weekend Ede would repair hers and anyone else's bicycle in the back yard. She was at her happiest fixing things.

One time Mam tried to teach Ede to knit. Ede was all fingers and thumbs and declared why should she need to know how to knit. It seemed odd that those same fingers and thumbs could put anything mechanical back together with lightning speed and dexterity.

I bet, after giving birth to two boys, Mam would have been overjoyed to have a daughter. I would also like to bet she would never have dreamt Ede would turn out to be the tomboy that she was.

Hazel Stevens

3 - Our Baby Sister

When Dad married Mam she moved into Dad's family home, number one Congleton Terrace, with Grandpa and Nana Wagstaff. Mam says she got on famously with them. In those days when money was short this is often what young couples did. A lot still do nowadays. In Mam and Dad's case this is where they remained.

Grandpa Wagstaff died, before I was born, Mam was pregnant with Ike at the time. Nana passed away just a few months later. Mam said, Grandpa Wagstaff had consumption as he used to work in the asbestos factory on Main Road. She told me Nana Wagstaff died of a broken heart as they had been together since they were fourteen. Childhood sweethearts we would say now, but in their time they weren't children as they were both working twelve hour days.

When Mam went into hospital to have Our Ede we, our Ike and me, went to stay with Mam's parents. They used to live in the next street, Horsley Road, until Granddad retired from the mill and they bought a bungalow on the edge of Leeds. It was a corner one and had garden round three sides. I loved staying with Granny and Granddad, they spoilt us both. It was great to be able to walk out of the back door into a real garden. Vegetables of every different kind grew there and all the passers by admired Granddad's roses in the front garden.

I missed Mam though while she was in hospital having Ede. What was taking her so long? I couldn't understand when Granny said she had to rest. Mam seemed to have been away forever. At last Granny and Granddad had gone to bring Mam and the new baby home. Our Ike seemed unusually quiet that day and wouldn't play with me. It seemed to take them ages to bring Mam home but they finally arrived and we ran into the bungalow. We had been next door where kind Auntie Gladys had given us pop and biscuits. She wasn't our real Auntie, just a friend of the family, what you would call a courtesy Auntie. Quite a few of Mam and Dad's friends were our Aunts and Uncles. Mam said it was more polite and respectful than us children just calling them by their first names. She was right of course. What's that saying? 'Familiarity breeds contempt'. Could this be why some youngsters these days have less respect for their elders than we used to have and still do? Oh I'd better not go all political had I?

Anyway Auntie Gladys tried to keep us amused, I guess she found Ike hard going, he sat on the sofa looking at nothing, saying nothing. I tried to get him to play a game of Snap, but he was having none of it and wouldn't even tell me what was wrong. He'd drunk two glasses of pop, so I told Auntie Gladys, I thought he must have the belly ache.

A frown of grave concern furrowed the old lady's brow. She perched next to Ike and muttered words of sympathy. I remember him blushing red at her embrace and him telling her there was 'nowt wrong'. I knew there was but he wasn't going to tell me or Auntie Gladys, so we went on playing Snap without him.

Ten little fingers and ten little toes, they were all there. I counted them just to make sure. I stared down at the heart shaped faced and thought how small Our Ede was, Mam had tears in her eyes as Ike and I looked at our new baby sister for the first time.

'It's a girl.' Ike said rather sharply, as if he didn't know.

'Yes.' Mam nodded, I wondered what difference it would make. I knew Mam loved Ike and me, she had such a lot of love, more than enough to share with our baby sister. So I decided it wouldn't make any difference. Besides there were several kids in our street who had sisters and they seemed to get on okay. I bent over Ede and placed my finger in the palm of her hand, she curled her tiny fingers round it and held it tightly. Mam beamed with delight at the smile I gave her.

'I'm sorry you couldn't come to the hospital,' Mam told us, 'they wouldn't let children in the wards.' She added.

Granddad started to laugh and pretty soon we all joined in, though at the time I couldn't understand why we were laughing. Guess now it was because it was the Maternity Hospital and what else do they have there other than children!

We stayed on at Granddad's for two more weeks. Granny fussed round Mam and Ede so much I was glad to get into the garden with Granddad.

'You'll make a grand gardener,' he would say, his blue eyes twinkling down at me. Ike didn't want to garden, he just trundled up and down the street outside on a make shift go-cart Granddad's pal had brought round for us. Ike would shout at me to play, but I ignored him, as when I did go out to him he made me pull the go-cart up and down the street. I never did have a ride on it.

I felt sad when we finally went home. I promised Granddad when I was old enough I would help him with his garden everyday after school. I didn't get the chance, my Granddad died when I was nine. Granny couldn't cope with the garden so she sold the bungalow and moved into a tiny flat in a tower block. I felt very sad the first time we went to visit and I looked out over the smoky city of Leeds.

'Where's Granddad?' I asked, waiting for him to bound in with mud on his boots and a cheery smile.

'Up there watching over all of us.' Granny said pointing to the sunbeams tumbling out from behind a cloud. It was then I remembered he had died and gone to heaven, I wasn't sure where that was, but I hoped it had a garden.

Ede grew quickly and began to notice things, she would smile and giggle as I ran out of school to meet her and my Mam. Ike was usually busy talking to his mates. I would always speak to Ede first and on the way home tell her and Mam about school. I loved school, at first thought I wouldn't, hearing Ike talk about bullies and sums. I couldn't wait to tell Ede and Mam all about my day.

I didn't even mind the sums, but reading was my favourite. I didn't get bullied either as Ike said I would. It didn't take me long to realise it was because Ike was my big brother and the lads in my class were scared of him.

Ike trailed behind us, I knew he thought he was too old to be met out of school. Mam told him firmly that it wasn't safe for him to come home on his own. The streets were getting increasingly busy.

The days grew shorter as autumn drew to a close. By Christmas Ede was sitting up and beaming at us all. She was chubby and long for her age. Mam would sit her on the floor amongst baby toys, but Ede would manage to move herself across to the coal scuttle. Every day she would end up covered in black coal dust. In sheer desperation Dad made an extended fire guard enclosing the scuttle inside it. Every day he declared what a tomboy Ede was going to be and he was sure she would get a job as a coal man or a miner. I asked how could she be a coal man when she was a girl. They all laughed at me and I remember feeling rather indignant.

It took Ike a long time to accept me in his room and I realised why he hadn't liked the idea of our new baby being a girl, because he had to share his room with me. I thought of all the things we could do as Mam tucked me into bed in Ike's room the night we all came home from Granddad's. While we had been away Dad had decorated my room in a bright pink, he had moved all my things into Ike's room there was still loads of space to set up Ike's train set. Ike flung himself onto his bed and moaned.

'Ike,' I whispered after Mam had left and put the light out, 'we will have some fun together won't we?'

Ike grumbled something I couldn't understand.

'What's wrong?' I whispered in the darkness. 'I don't mind sharing.'

'I do!' Ike said angrily.

'You do what?' I asked innocently.

'Mind sharing, this is my room! Why can't you share your room with her?' he snapped at me. I remember feeling frightened, Ike sounded so strange and angry.

'But,' I explained slowly, 'girls can't share bedrooms with boys. Mam told us.'

Ike didn't speak, he turned over in bed and lay facing the wall.

It took Ike a long time to come round and accept Our Ede. I know now how pushed out and jealous he must have felt. You see I was the one who would go down to the allotment garden Dad had off Cemetery Road. I went with him as soon as I could walk, every Saturday. Ike stayed at home with Mam and when we came home tired and muddy for tea, Ike would chatter away about what a grand time he and Mam had baking, shopping or visiting our Great Aunt Eliza. Now all this had come to an end and Ike knew Ede would always be with them. I heard Mam tell Dad one Saturday night that Ike hadn't been in all afternoon, he been round at Sid Cartwright's. Sid, the older brother of my school pal Joe. Mam said Sid was really cheeky and she didn't know if she wanted Ike round there.

'They're just kids Lib,' Dad said firmly. 'They'll be fine, it could be worse he could be hanging a round with the Listers. You know last week when the oldest one Tom had been nicked for breaking into the post office? Well, it seems...' Dad dropped his voice so I never did hear any more.

It wasn't until Our Ede was just over a year old and whereas most kids usually say Dad or Mam as their first words, Our Ede clapped her hands with delight one Saturday when Ike came back from Sid's and she shouted, 'Ike, Ike.' It was as clear as anything. Ike just stood and stared at her. After she said it again he went up to her and picked her up. Mam was about to remind him to be careful when she stopped herself and smiled at Dad and me. Ede was holding onto Ike's hair as he cuddled her. She pulled harder and he screamed loudly in pain. Ede gave a little giggle in that moment, somehow, a friendship was formed. After a year of feeling jealous Ike suddenly became very protective of her. Ede found she could wind him round her little finger and practically get away with anything. I guessed this was why Ike hadn't gone mad when she had messed around with his motorbike. At nearly six I found it most confusing after hearing Ike moan on about Ede when we went to bed, now he would tell me in great detail how she had done this and done that.

Dad called Ede his little princess. She was christened Ede Ann one fine October Sunday. Maybe when she started walking she would get in less mess and could wear the carefully hand sewn dresses Mam sat each night making. Trimming them with lace and smocking the bodices. She was very clever at sewing was Mam. Her daughter would be beautiful, just as they said Princess Ann was, dainty and pretty. She couldn't have got Our Ede more wrong.

By the time Ede started school Mam had almost given up dressing her in the pretty frocks everyday. Ede would snag them on something or get them covered in mud or even worse oil. When she was at home I often found Ede dressed in my old dungarees and shorts. The only way you could tell she was a girl was by the long hair which Mam battled to plait every day. There were awful rows when Ede started school. It seemed every day she came home with torn muddy clothes because she had been playing football with some older lads. I would cringe if I saw her as I knew my mates would rib me about her.

Even now Joe reminds me of how, when she was seven, Ede squared up to Sadie Lister who was eleven and like me just about to leave Mill Street School. It seems Sadie was bragging about how her sister Joan had kissed our Ike behind the bike sheds at the secondary school they both went to. Ede didn't like what she was hearing so had pushed Sadie Lister over, she then sat on top of Sadie and beat her with her fists until Miss Brown came and dragged her off. Mam was called into the Head's office when she came to collect us. I had to wait outside. Mam sent Ede to bed that night straight after her tea. Later on after I had gone upstairs Mam had a right old go at Ike and told him he hadn't to have any more to do with the Lister family. Ike was furious when he came upstairs, I asked him if it was true and had he kissed Joan Lister. He denied it flatly but I didn't believe him. A few weeks later I saw Joan Lister with her arm round Tommy Shillitoe, so wondered if Ike had perhaps been telling the truth.

Ike thought he was really handsome back then. His dark hair slicked back with Brylcream, tight drain pipe trousers and a daft shoe lace hanging round the neck of his open shirt. A stream of girls would knock on the door for him or hang around outside just to catch a glimpse. It was sickening really. Yes, perhaps I was jealous as no girls called for me or hung around outside. Not that I would have wanted them to anyway. Later on of course I had Mrs Rowntree, she was the only female I wanted in my life then apart from Mam that is and I suppose our Ede. The latter of course drove me mad but we all loved her.

Hazel Stevens

4 - Changes

After the episode with Sadie Lister I was glad to leave Mill Street School and go to Hillside Secondary School. Thankful to be in different class from Sadie who, since Ede flew at her, had been giving me really awful looks. I was scared in case she set her older brothers on me. Margaret Lister had seven children in the first seven years of her marriage. Tom was a couple of years older than Ike, then came Joan, Billy, Harry, Sadie the same age as me, Dennis a year younger than me and finally Phyllis two years younger than me. Phyllis was different from the others, quieter, and I remember Our Ede laughing at the way Phyllis always had her head in some fairy story or other.

Phyllis was thin, with long blond hair and enormous blue eyes. The others were tall for their ages and very heavily built. Phyllis just didn't seem to belong to the same family.

I loved Hillside School, there was so much more to do. It meant going to different classrooms for different lessons. Whenever Joe and I met up with Ike he would always send us the wrong way, we'd then be in trouble for being late to class. Joe's brother Sid heard we were having trouble finding our way round so became our guide when he could.

But best of all they had a garden, once a week we

had a lesson teaching us how to garden. Mr Butcher, the teacher who took the lesson, was wonderful. He knew lots about gardening nearly as much as my Granddad did. I loved those lessons. I was thrilled when he started a special lunchtime gardening club. It wasn't long before I spent all my lunchtimes in the greenhouse or in the vegetable plot.

In my last year there Mr Butcher commandeered me and I helped out with the first years and when they had their gardening lesson. I think it was Mr Butcher who had a hand in getting me the job at Warrens Nursery. The year after I left school Ede told me Mr Butcher had a heart attack and they found him dead amongst the cabbages. The school decided to take gardening off the timetable and it wasn't long before the garden and greenhouse had been replaced with two mobile classrooms. I felt sad, I owed a lot to Mr Butcher. Felt sad too the school had lost it's garden. Like the rest of Leeds, any green space seemed to being built on. People called it the sprawling city and I knew they were right.

In the fifties and sixties Leeds grew at a tremendous rate. Mills were closing and some pulled down to make way for tiny box like homes. Some left empty for years and years until they were eventually renovated and turned into flats. Everyone marvelled at the immense structure being built close to the centre, bright airy, concrete and steel, they were going to call it The Merrion Centre. It was going to have shops, offices, bowling alley, car parking and several pubs. It finally opened in 1964. Joe, myself and a few others went along to have a look after it opened and had a go at ten pin bowling, but it was too closed in and busy for me. Joe kept going bowling for quite a while, until he was older, then he took up bowling outside on a green. Much more sensible though I, despite Joe's requests, have never taken up bowling up myself.

Horsley Road had become really rough, with youths hanging round the small off licence on the corner. Mam told us to keep away, she was frightened of them. What Mam didn't know was, they were frightened of Ike, and wouldn't have harmed any of his family at any price. Congleton Terrace kept itself neat and tidy. Many of the residents having been born there and they continued to keep it as their parents had done before them.

A lot of people blamed the foreigners in Horsley Road for its demise. It wasn't long before Pakistanis, Africans and Indians were living side by side. Some said they came from mud huts and didn't know how to look after a proper house. After visiting our school pals, Isher and Raj from Africa and India, Joe and I knew people were talking out of their hats. Their homes were beautiful, the walls covered in brightly coloured rugs and wall hangings. I told Mam you could eat your dinner off Raj's floor and she laughed and said, 'Don't tell your Granny you've been round there.' Even Granny's old house looked smart, the windows painted bright blue and a lovely red front door. A Chinese family moved in there and though I didn't really know them, they seemed okay.

What all the fuss was about I just don't know. People are people after all and did it really matter what colour skin they had. Mum kept tight lipped about it all but Dad aired his views quite regularly, though even he had to admit that the men and women of ethnic origin who worked in the factory under him were 'damn good workers'. After a while he regarded them as friends too and would often meet up with them in the working man's club for a drink. Black or white the workers at the mill all respected my Dad and when I was out with him, I noticed they would always speak.

'Morning Mr Wagstaff, morning Master Wagstaff.' I felt proud to be with my Dad and hear the genuine regard they had for him and me. Yes, in those days Leeds was becoming very much a multicultural city. This did cause problems for many of the immigrants. It was sad to see so much racism and hatred, and as I said before people are people and all the same. Though I think perhaps it was a lot to do with religion and people's ignorance of others way of life. Perhaps jealousy too as many of our new neighbours worked hard and spent little so soon became affluent.

Remember I told you our Ike went down to London to work. Well the day he left Mam and Ede were inconsolable, their eyes red and puffy with crying. I couldn't see myself what all the fuss was about. Ike left in the early hours of Monday morning, and whilst he was training, he would be home again on Friday night. Mam of course worried about the conflicts between the black and white population in London which was worse than Leeds. She refused to have her fears allayed when Dad told her most of the problems were round the Brixton area and miles from where our Ike was. For the next few months though Ike would only be working Monday to Friday and be home by train, which took hours from London to Leeds in those days. It only takes less than two nowadays.

Mam would get up at four in the morning to see Ike off for the early train on Mondays. On Friday, tea would be delayed until Ike arrived home. He'd dump his washing, bolt his tea and be off down the local boozer with his mates.

'Coming 'Am?' he'd often ask.

'Indeed he is not Isaac Wagstaff!' Mam would chide, 'Get yerself away, you know Sam's not old enough!'

I knew I wasn't but just sometimes I did think that I would like to say 'no' to Ike myself. I didn't want to hang around with his crowd and the group of giggling girls who seemed to follow Ike and his mates round like sheep. Yes, I would like to tell him so myself instead of our Mam jumping in all the time. Ike would go off laughing.

'One day,' he'd say. One day I did think it might happen and when I was old enough he might persuade me to join him on a Friday night at the local or even on a Saturday night round the city centre pubs and even the night clubs. Ike went to them all often rolling in at three or four in the morning. Trying hard not to wake everyone up, but he usually did. I'd hear Dad hollering at him, before Ike stumbled into his bed and in an instant fall into a deep sleep, snoring his head off. I covered my head with my pillow, but it always took me ages to get back to sleep.

It never did happen me going out on the town with Ike, as just a few short months later he met Lily. His visits home at weekends grew less and less. After he had done his training he had to work weekends anyway. So we were lucky if we saw him once every three months. After the wedding it became 'once in a blue moon' that Ike and Lily would venture north.

Mam and Ede, however, often went down to visit him and Ede would come back full of the adventures she had going out with Ike. He took her on the underground, even to the engine depot. His mate Vic was an engineer on the trains, he'd had been really impressed by Ede's mechanical knowledge and she thought how lucky Vic was to be doing such a good job. I shook my head in disbelief, give me the outside life any day.

Ede became more and more interested in how machines worked and I would often see her, on a Saturday, with Sadie Lister round at the garage where Sadie's brother Tom worked. Ede and Sadie had somehow become friends, after the carry on over Ike and Sadie's sister Joan. I could not understand that, as at the time, Ede hated Sadie!

Ede would come home starry eyed and rush upstairs to get rid of the grease and oil stains before Dad came in. I knew he would not approve of her hanging round with any of the Listers. I could never tell though, whether she was starry eyed cos she'd spent a day in a garage, or starry eyed because of Tom Lister, I prayed it wasn't the latter.

One day Joe said, 'Ede is turning into a right looker.'

I was disgusted and told him so. Still his comment made me look at Ede in a different light. Ede was changing, gone had the gangly frame of a tomboy. She was tall now and slim. Her long hair always tied back, in a high ponytail as she called it. She still moaned about wearing skirts for school, as the rest of the time she wore trousers, slacks she called them. They seemed to hug her figure and she often got wolf whistles as she walked down the street, her pony tail swinging to and fro.

One evening we were huddled round the fire. The nights were drawing in and there was an early October frost. Mam had just returned from a parents evening at Ede's school. 'Alf, Ede's teachers told me Ede's a great help at school. She repaired Mr Ashton's bike one day and Mrs. Cook's sewing machine another.'

'Good, good,' Dad replied nonchalantly, his head still in the Evening Post.

'Alf,' Mam went on, 'Mr Burke, the head, told me she'd fixed his car.'

'Oh no Ede! Not the head teacher's car, you didn't.' Dad burst out glaring across the room at my sister. Who, up until his outburst, had been sitting with a smug grin on her face. Even I cringed at Dad's voice and at my sister actually helping the 'Right Proper Burk' as we had nick named the head of Hillside Secondary.

'Calm down Alf, his car is fine.' Mam said sternly. Dad relaxed a little in his chair and began to read the paper again. Mam smiled encouragingly at Ede and then dropped the bombshell. 'Mr. Burke says Ede has an unusual talent for a girl and she should be encouraged to do something about it.'

'Mmm.' mumbled Dad turning to the sports page.

'Mr Burke said Ede could go to college.' Mam pressed on gently.

'Mmm, good.' mumbled Dad again.

'Yes, to do mechanical engineering.' Mam announced with a proud flourish.

Dad and I jerked our heads and looked from one to the other female members of our family. They were grinning identically at Dad. I glanced at Dad and the look on his face caused me to catch my breath and the smiles vanished from Mam and Ede.

'My daughter will do no such thing!' Dad said, throwing his paper to the floor and staring at them both. 'Go to college yes, but to do shorthand or typing or whatever it is girls do! But whoever heard of a girl, doing mechanical engineering? Eh. Tell me!'

'Dad,' Ede wailed, 'I would really like to and I know I'd be good at it.'

'No!' Dad shouted, 'You would be a laughing stock.'

'But Dad...' Ede sat forward in her chair wringing her hands together. She did this when she was upset or frustrated about anything.

'I've spoken girl, now you will do as you are told and I won't hear any more of the nonsense about you going to college to do mechanical engineering. It's absurd! Do you hear me?' Dad glared, his face going red.

'I...I won't be,' stammered Ede close to tears. 'Why Sadie Lister is going to drive the buses as soon as she is allowed to, she says that time will come sooner or later.'

'You are not Sadie Lister!' Dad yelled across the room. 'That family let their kids run wild and I won't have their name mentioned in this house. You can get yourself to bed Ede. When the time comes for you to leave school we will discuss then which course you will do at Wharton College.'

'But Dad Wharton is for girls only. I don't want to go to Wharton I want to go to Farnley Hills. I can do mechan...' Ede's voice trailed off as Dad rose out of the chair.

'Bed girl. I will not be answered back!' He yelled at her, 'Bed now!' Ede fled upstairs and I followed. I had never seen Dad so enraged. I sensed Mam and Dad might have an argument so I hid on the landing just to make sure they didn't fall out. I should have known better. I heard them talking quietly for about five minutes, their voices were low and I couldn't make out what they were saying.

'Oh Alf, remember the War?' Mam said as she opened the door. I pressed back against the wall hoping she wouldn't see me.

'She'll be a laughing stock Lib. The War years were exceptional, everyone had to get their hands dirty, but

this is now and my daughter will be doing a proper job!'
Dad sighed as he turned the wireless on.

'Mmm,' Mam mumbled, 'Cuppa?' She went into the
kitchen and I heard the kettle going on. I turned and
walked along the landing to my bedroom. It was only
eight o'clock, but that morning I had bought the latest
gardening magazine and was keen to read it. I heard
Ede sobbing quietly as I approached her bedroom door.
I opened it cautiously, waiting for the all too familiar,
'Get out of my room.' Ede didn't yell that at me this
time, so I stepped into her pink domain. She lay face
down on the bright pink candlewick bedspread.

'It's OK Ede.' I whispered perching beside her.
'You'll find something to do.'

'I want to do mechanical engineering Am,' she said
flatly, turning over and wiping her face with the backs
of her hands.

'Girls can't do that.' I told her.

'Yes they can, Mr Burke said so, besides, I know I
can do it and I will do it so help me, somehow I will!' She
stared up at the ceiling and I knew there would be no
reasoning with her. I retreated to my room, closing the
door quietly behind me. It was my room, though Ike's
bed still remained, a dumping ground for my gardening magazines and clean clothes. But still my very own
room and I can't tell you how glad I was not to have to
share with Ike any more. I don't think he ever got over
having to share with me anyway after Ede arrived. We
got on okay I guess. But he hated the way I liked to
read in bed on a night. I hated the way, at weekends,

he would come stumbling home drunk and his snoring would keep me awake.

I missed him though. Especially after he met Lily and wasn't home so much. Yes, I really did miss him.

Hazel Stevens

5 - Ede's First Kiss

Ike, Lily and the kids came that Christmas. Ike made fun of Ede and her college aspirations, which only made matters worse. There had been an awful atmosphere between Dad and Ede since that night and try as he might Dad just didn't have the same rapport with his daughter as he had before.

Ede too had changed. She grew distant and more aloof. She started wearing make up, even when she was going down to the garage where Tom Lister worked. I worried, and half wondered whether to speak to Mam about where Ede went. Dad would be furious if he knew she spent her Saturdays in the company of a Lister and in a garage too! He assumed she was at Lucy Braithwaite's. As before, Dad spent all day on the allotment or going to see Leeds Rugby. I worked every Saturday now so couldn't go with him. I missed the closeness we shared at those rugby matches and on the allotment. Mam still went to Harrogate to see Great Aunt Eliza.

After the incident with Ike's motorbike, Mam started taking Ede with her, until Ede became so tiresome and complained there was nothing to do. Mam agreed to Ede spending time with Lucy and she did for several months until Lucy was dropped and Ede formed the friendship with Sadie Lister. Phyllis would be with them too. I'd see them hanging around the shops on my way home from work. Catching sight of me Ede would wave me down, begging me to promise not to tell Mam or Dad who I'd seen her with. I would nod my oath and look very serious, so she knew I wouldn't tell them. It's strange the bond between siblings. How they cover each other tracks so willingly. Even though if it ever comes to light, you are in as much trouble for keeping their secret, as I knew Ede and I would be if Dad found out she was hanging round with a Lister and I knew about it.

I always spoke to Phyllis and the shy girl would smile, whilst keeping her eyes glued to the pavement. Sadie didn't speak to me. Never has done since she had the fight with Our Ede, I thought it most strange that they should become friends now.

That Christmas, with Ike, Lily and all four kids, it was rather a full house. Buddy seemed to do nothing but howl.

'Teething.' Lily said as she pouted and petted over him.

Ike brought the college subject up again in front of Dad. He said how Ede had worked with his mate on some of the underground trains when she had stayed with them during the October half term.

'Right impressed with her, Vic was, Dad.' He told him. 'Vic said she has quite a natural talent for it.'

'I don't care what Vic said, whoever Vic might be. My daughter will be going to do shorthand and typing at Wharton College for a year. There will then be a job for her at the mill in the finance office.' Dad said proudly.

'No.' Ede stood up from the kitchen table where we had all been sitting just finishing our Christmas dinner. I swallowed hard just thinking it had not been a bad Christmas despite the howling Buddy. Dad looked up at Ede and asked her to sit down. 'No!' She repeated loudly, staring around helplessly for some back up. Silently we looked from her to Dad. Shirley began to whimper. Frankie and Conway stared at Ede in horror. They had never heard her raise her voice.

'I won't do it!' She said firmly.

'Won't do what Ede?' Asked Dad, a grin fixed on his face.

'Won't go to college, to do bloody shorthand and typing!' Ede declared defiantly. Dad's smile vanished in an instant and we all gasped.

'Don't you dare use language like that in this house!' Dad hollered, shoving his chair back, he reached his hand out towards her face.

'Alf, no!' Our Mam grabbed his wrist, tears filled her eyes. Dad sat back down looking defeated for a moment. Ede looked terrified and about to flee.

'Sorry Dad,' she mumbled into her lap, 'I just don't want to do shorthand and typing at college,' she looked up expectantly.

'OK, then you can come to the mill and I am sure they will take you on as an office junior.' Dad told her.

For a second Ede glared at him, jumped up from her seat, marched out of the kitchen grabbing her coat on the way past. She slammed the back door and the back gate behind her. Dad rose to go after her, I knew he disapproved strongly of her behaviour. Mam put her hand on his arm.

'Leave it Alf, let her calm down.' She whispered. 'It's another seven months before she leaves school, we will discuss it then.'

'There will be nothing to discuss Lib!' Dad remonstrated loudly, at which point the momentary silent Buddy decided to howl louder. Mam and Lily's attention were given to him and Ike, much to my relief, distracted Dad by talking about Leeds Rugby. They were soon back to the genial bantering of rugby versus football and I buried my head in the brilliant gardening book Great Aunt Eliza had sent me. I read the same page twice, when I realised I wasn't really reading at all just wondering where Ede had gone and if she was okay. I thought she may have gone to Lucy's, but realistically I knew she would be knocking on the Lister's door. I can only guess at what happened next.

Ede was relieved when Tom answered the door. He saw her tear stained face and wrapped his big arms around her, softly kissing away the tears. His lips caressed her cheeks before finding her lips. It was Ede's first kiss and she was so glad it was Tom. He was very gentle and coaxed her into returning his kiss with a passion Ede had never felt before or even could understand. She laid her head on his muscular chest and openly declared her love for him. Tom laughed and told her he loved her too. Tom thought this young girl was a marvel by the way she seemed to share his love for

motors.

He drew Ede into the Lister's living room, it was full of a laughing family enjoying their time together at Christmas. Ede loved being part of this, and they willingly shuffled round to make room for her to sit beside Sadie.

Sadie was still in her uniform, having been working on the omnibuses round Leeds town centre as a bus conductress.

Ede thought the Lister's were a wonderful family, none of them worried about what people would say, even when their Dad was sent down for pinching lead off the church roof. Ede's own family had been horrified to read about him in the paper. But here he was just out and welcomed back to his family as if he'd been on holiday.

Sadie had been given every encouragement by her family to do what she wanted to. Why, oh why couldn't Ede's family be the same?

'One day.' Sadie had told her. 'Men and women will do the same jobs like they did in the War. What short memories people have. Only when it happens this time they will also get the same pay for doing it.'

Although Sadie loved her job, it angered her that men doing the same job were getting paid a lot more than she was. This would irk Ede too and she wondered if mechanical engineers were paid differently. She was determined to find out and later as Tom kissed her again in the alleyway outside the back gate of number one Congleton Terrace, she asked him what he thought about her going to Farnley Hills.

Tom lifted her up and swung her round. 'You'll be a first class mechanic my Ede. I've told you though Old Man Swinley might give you a job as my apprentice at the garage. We'll have some fun eh?' He kissed her again and for the next few moments she was lost in the smell of his aftershave and the beer he'd been drinking. When he pulled her to him, she found she was panting a little, again experiencing feelings she couldn't understand. She felt very light headed and thought it must be the sherry Mrs Lister had pressed her to drink. Ede told Tom she didn't want to be just a mechanic, she wanted to design and build cars, machines and engines.

'OK my little one, you're the boss. See you Saturday.' Tom laughed. Ede nodded. Today was Tuesday and Saturday seemed so far away. Tom dropped a kiss on her forehead, turned and was gone, Ede leant against the wall still feeling the pressure of his lips on hers and his strong arms around her. She shivered and realised it wasn't because she was cold.

Reluctantly, she turned and opened the back gate ready to face the music. Slipping in through the back door Ede was relieved to find her Mam, Lily and me, surrounded by three laughing children. Buddy was fast asleep in Dad's armchair and the rest of them were playing with wooden building bricks on the floor. Dad and Ike were nowhere to be seen.

'It's OK Ede, yer Dad and Ike have gone to the club for a pint. 'There's tea in the pot.' Mam said softly, smiling with relief that her daughter was home and safe.

Ede nodded and went into the kitchen, 'Anyone else for tea?' She asked. Mam and I nodded.

'Yes please,' Lily said, 'I'll give you a hand.'

Inside the kitchen Ede busied herself getting out four cups and saucers. It being Christmas Day the best crockery was always used. Lily passed Ede the milk from the pantry. We didn't have a fridge in those days, just a large walk in larder with a great big stone shelf to keep things cool. Lily kept her hand on the bottle, as Ede reached for it. Ede looked at her startled.

'Who is he?' Lily whispered as she let go of the bottle.

'What? What are you talking about?' Ede said through gritted teeth, but a bright pink flush crept into her face.

'The bloke?' Lily insisted, with a slight smirk.

'No one!'

'Oh come on Ede, it stands out a mile you've been snogging somebody.' Lily smiled triumphantly.

'What if I have!' Ede's hands shook as she poured the tea.

'No reason, but I bet yer Dad won't like it.'

'You won't tell him or Mam or Ike...will you?' Ede's face paled as she stared desperately at Lily.

'Not if you don't want me to.' Lily shrugged. 'It's nothing to me.' Taking two cups Lily went back into the living room, leaving Ede pale and shaken because not only had someone discovered her secret, but she'd even confessed it. Lily must have seen her and Tom in the back alley. Gulping down the hot tea, Ede tried to calm herself down. If Dad found out about Tom Lister there really would be hell to pay and that would be no mistake.

'Think I'll go to bed Mam,' Ede said, passing me a cup of tea, I noticed her hands were trembling.

'OK love, you do look pale, doesn't she Lily?' Mam said gently. Lily nodded and winked at Ede.

'Say tara to our Ike won't you, is it okay if I come down in the February half term Lily?' Ede asked carefully.

'If you're on your own that's fine by me.' Lily replied smugly. 'Unless you're coming Mam?' She added quickly.

'Of course I'll be on my own.' Ede snapped and flounced out of the room.

'Yes, she will be on her own.' Mam told Lily. 'I have promised to take Aunt Eliza to see cousin Nora for a day or two that week. It will be good to know Ede is with you.'

'Oh yes, Ike will make sure she behaves herself.' Lily grinned.

'Of course Ede will behave herself Lily.' Mam couldn't understand why her daughter-in-law found this all so amusing.

I sat and stared at Lily's wide grin, I'd never seen her smile so much.

Buddy woke and yet again began to howl. Lily plucked him roughly from the armchair and demanded to know when Ike would be back, as they really should be setting off back to London. It seemed her demands were instantly granted as Ike and Dad appeared through the front door. The children were bustled into Ike's an old estate car that replaced the Ford and the family were gone leaving behind a very quiet household.

Dad plopped into his chair and nodded as Mam told him Ede was in bed. Dad grimaced a little. The two pints of beer with whisky chasers, he'd drank whilst out with Ike, had mellowed him, he lay back in the chair and closed his eyes. It wasn't long before the deep regular breathing indicated he was asleep.

I smiled at Mam and gathered up the cups. Yes apart from the incident with Our Ede, it hadn't been a bad Christmas Day. I put the milk back in the larder and vowed I would save up and buy Mam a fridge. It was the sixties after all. Yet, apart from the electric kettle, this house hadn't changed much since Mam moved in there over twenty years before. It was time for some changes. Dad seemed reluctant to make them but I would. It would make our Mam's life a bit easier. I rinsed the cups and left them by the sink. Taking my gardening book, I whispered goodnight to Mam and gave her a hug. She looked up and smiled, I noticed her eyes looked tired. I hugged her tighter.

'It'll be okay Mam.' I whispered and when she finally nodded, I let her go and went off to my bed.

6 - A Family Divided

One evening in the middle of January as we were just settling down after tea the telephone rang in the hall. Mam, Dad and I looked at each other questioningly, as if one of us knew who was calling. The loud jangling of the bell had made Mam jump. She was relieved when the telephone was installed not long after Ike left to work in London. It did mean he could ring home regularly and Mam didn't have to rely on letters to know if he was okay. Give Ike his due he rang home once a week, usually on a Sunday. This was a Wednesday, not Sunday, and as Ike was, nearly always, the only person to ring us, we were all wondering who it could be. Dad smiled at our puzzled expressions and got up out of the chair to answer it.

After a short conversation, Dad came back into the living room and beckoned Mam. All Ede and I could hear was urgent muffled talking. We wondered what on earth could be wrong.

Mam soon put us out of our misery when she and Dad came back into the room. In a stunned voice Mam explained. It was Ike calling, to tell us Lily had not only left him, she had also abandoned her children too. It seemed she had run off with one of Ike's so called friends. Ike didn't know where. Mam said he sounded in a 'right state'.

She immediately went upstairs to pack a bag, to catch the next train to London. Dad tried to protest.

Mam was firm, she was going to London and that was that.

Dad, Ede and I watched solemnly as a taxi whisked Mam away. I turned to look at Ede, surprised to see great tears rolling down her face.

'It's okay Ede, Ike and the kids will be okay. Mam will sort it out.' I put an arm round her shoulder.

'It's not that, j...j...just how long will Mam be away?' Ede stammered and gulped back the tears.

'She said she may be gone a couple of weeks.' Dad spoke quietly sounding very forlorn. 'I'm going to the pub.' With that he walked off down the street, leaving Ede and I staring after him.

I pulled Ede into the house, she was still sobbing. I pushed her into a chair at the kitchen table. For some reason I put the kettle on and made some tea. Guess it's what I've seen Mam do a thousand times in stressful situations. I still don't know if a cuppa calms the stressed person down or just gives time for the person dealing with it something to do and time to think.

Ede took the cuppa with shaking hands and drank deeply. I sipped mine. With my free hand I steadied Ede's cup so she wouldn't spill her tea.

'What's wrong Ede?' It seemed a strange question for me to ask under the circumstances. But somehow I guessed Ede's tears weren't because of Lily leaving Ike. That it was somehow because Mam was going to be with Ike for a couple of weeks.

Ede stared up at me with the same sad eyes I had seen when she took Ike's bike to bits.

'D...D...Dad,' she stammered. 'He won't agree, he won't sign and...and it has to be there next week.'

'What has?' I felt very confused.

'Me...me application form for college,' she cried.

'Course Dad will sign it, don't be daft. I will ask him.' I realised now the reason for Ede's tears. Even though we didn't say any more, we both knew the importance of all this. I knew sparks would be flying over Dad signing the college form. He just wouldn't agree, we both knew that. Now it was down to me to try and persuade him.

Mam rang on the Saturday morning. Ike was feeling more positive and the children were fine. Mam would be staying down there until something could be sorted out. Dad shook his head as he told us this. He mumbled something about how he knew Ike would pay for marrying Lily.

'Dad,' I took a deep breath, I already knew what the answer would be. But I promised I would ask. 'Ede needs her forms signed for Farnley Hills.'

'What lad, what are you talking about?' Dad glared at me and I could feel Ede shrink behind me.

'Farnley Hills.' I repeated slowly.

'You mean Wharton, where are they Ede?' He asked firmly.

'I knew it would be no good.' Ede yelled and flounced out of the house, slamming the door behind her.

I just stared blankly and shrugged when Dad asked what all that was about. He looked pretty mad and I knew it was because of the door slamming. However a little later, when he appeared calmer. I plucked up courage.

'Dad, you know Our Ede has her heart set on Farnley Hills, to do engineering.' I said quietly, sitting down opposite Dad in Mam's chair.

'She ain't got to you too with her stupid ideas, has she?' He put the paper down and sighed.

'I don't think it's so stupid Dad.' I said boldly and immediately regretted it.

Dad flung the paper on the floor, 'Now look 'ere lad,' he began, leaning forward in his chair. 'As I told yer Mam, it's senseless Our Ede getting new fangled ideas. For the last time I am not gonna be a laughing stock. Ede goes to Wharton or into the Mill.' He sat back in his chair as if giving me time to digest what he had just said. 'Look at it like this Sam, you'll know when you have your own family. Girls do office jobs, keep house and stuff like that. Before you know it Edith will be married and a couple of nippers hanging off her apron strings. By the way lad, you any feelers out in that direction?' He gave me a huge wink. 'No harm in a lad sowing a few wild oats before he's tied down, know what I mean?'

I stared at him horrified, I had no intention of sowing any wild oats. I took a couple of deep breaths and ploughed on. 'Dad, Ede has her heart set on it you know and she is real good with machines and engines.' I knew I was digging myself in deeper.

Dad half rose out of the chair and glowered at me, 'I said no lad, are you as deaf as your sister? It's all that Sadie Lister's fault, a girl wanting to drive buses! When has she been speaking to her anyway? Damn the Listers! Nowt but trouble the lot of them!' Dad stopped short and sat back in his chair. 'Hadn't you better be getting to work?' He added, nodding to the old clock on the mantle piece. It was no good arguing further, this much I knew. Once Dad made his mind up about something there was no changing it for anyone. I wanted to remind him all that girls and women did, not so long ago, during the War years. But with the look on his face I decided it best to keep quiet.

No guesses where Ede would be go. Down to the garage where Tom Lister worked. Our Ede had quite a crush on him. I'd seen the pair of them together the week before. Tom was laughing and joking with her, I knew to remonstrate with her would only fan the flames of Ede's crush. I decided then I would be there for her when he broke Our Ede's heart. I wondered if he had a girl friend, good looking bloke like Tom Lister must have loads. Yet Ede was the only girl I saw hanging round the garage. Well except for Sadie who generally had Phyllis with her. As I've said before, Phyllis was so different and as she grew older she blossomed, the way her blonde hair framed her face made her look like an angel.

I pulled on my coat, 'Off to work now Dad.' I told him. He nodded and reached for the seed catalogue, planning for the allotment. 'I can get you seeds from work.' I reminded him, as I had done for the last three years. I noticed for the first time that morning his dark hair had a peppering of grey through it. Why hadn't I noticed that before?

Dad nodded and we both knew the seeds would come through the post from Darby's as they always did.

Pushing my bike into the alley, I glanced at my watch and turned to go the opposite way to work. Just time to go and check on Ede. I felt responsible for her with Mam being away. I just wish she wasn't quite so stubborn and headstrong, clashing out of the house as she did.

The garage was silent when I arrived, the big doors open wide. I propped my bike against them and stepped inside.

'Ede you here?' I said raising my voice a little and peering into the gloom. There was no reply. 'Tom, Tom Lister?' The workshop was eerily silent. I jumped as a hand came down gently on my shoulder.

'S...S...Sorry,' Phyllis Lister said softly as I turned to look at her. 'I...I didn't mean to make you jump.'

'It's OK.' I said feeling my face burning. In that instant for some strange reason I thought Phyllis Lister was more beautiful, more angelic than Mrs. Rowntree could ever be. I wanted to kiss those rosebud lips.

'Have you seen Our Ede?' I asked this angel.

'No, I came to bring our Tom's dinner,' she said holding out a battered biscuit tin. She looked round the garage. 'Tom,' she called. 'You here?'

'What's up?' Tom Lister asked as he came out of a room at the back of the workshop. Ede followed him, her face flushed and happy as she gazed up at him.

'Ede?' I asked, my throat dry, as I realised why she may have been looking so flushed. She wouldn't, not with Tom Lister. I stared helplessly from one to the other. Gulping swiftly, thoughts of Dad's reaction flashed through my mind.

'Sam?' Ede's happy smile faded as she saw my face and instantly realised I knew she was having a relationship with Tom Lister. She ran past an astonished Phyllis, grabbed me and pulled me outside. 'You won't tell Dad,' she cried through gritted teeth. Tears welling in her eyes.

'Ede, you and Tom Lister.' I hissed. 'How could you?'

'What, what do you mean?' She asked innocently.

'What you been up to?' I accused.

'Nothing, nothing.'

'Oh come on Ede, I wasn't born yesterday!'

'Sam, nothing, honest!' She stared at me with her big baleful eyes. 'We were only kissing.'

I grabbed my bike, shocked to the core at what she was saying. Our Ede kissing Tom Lister. With one hand on my bike I reached out the other and pushed her away. I needed to be at work, I needed the fresh country air. I pedalled away completely unaware that Tom, Ede and Phyllis were standing in the street watching me.

I reached work in my fastest time ever, the journey there went by unnoticed. My mind whirled with thoughts of Our Ede, Tom Lister and Phyllis. The latter I knew I would have to put out of my mind. It was a catastrophe that I knew Ede was infatuated by a Lister. I would not allow myself to even go there.

Through the morning my resolve faded several times as Phyllis popped into my head. I immediately shook myself and got on with my work of pricking out early seedlings. What on earth was matter with me? Yet there she came again and again. That angelic face, the halo of blonde hair, smiling so sweetly with perfectly shaped rosebud lips, I so wanted to kiss. Her slim lithe body I wanted to hold against me. I felt stirrings I've no wish to relate. I turned my thoughts to Dad. He hated the Lister family, all of them, he called them scroungers and layabouts. Fred Lister hadn't done a days work in his life, apparently. In my childhood I couldn't see how this was possible. As I grew older I would see his wife, Mrs Lister, dragging her thin weary body home from the mill, she looked worn out. I heard Dad telling Mam that Mrs Lister worked three hours overtime every night.

'What sort of man, even though he's in and out of the nick, sits by while his wife does that?' Dad would add sneeringly. Mam would shake her head and look sad.

Most of the Lister children were no better than their Dad, loud mouthed and idle. Dad was furious when one of the men at the mill asked if Ike and Sadie Lister were courting.

Ike laughed it off but I knew he was afraid of Dad. 'Wouldn't touch her with a barge pole.' Ike had vowed to our parents.

Dad believed him and settled down again. I think Dad was relieved Ike went to London out of Sadie's way.

What would Dad say if he knew about Ede and Tom Lister? Why she was a child and he was a grown man. My feelings for Phyllis, whatever they were, would have to stay in my head. No one would ever know how I was feeling about this beautiful, gorgeous girl. I stared ahead of me and closed my eyes, imagining she was close, standing right here in the greenhouse in front of me, I sighed deeply.

'It must be love,' a deep silky voice snapped my eyes open and I could feel myself turning crimson. I coughed loudly, to hide my embarrassment.

'Who is she?' Sighed Mrs Rowntree. I had been so wrapped up with my thoughts I didn't hear her come into the greenhouse. 'Sam, I need to know my competition,' she added, beaming mischievously at me.

'I...I don't...don't know what you're talking about.' I stammered out, my face burning with embarrassment.

'It's OK Sam, I'm only teasing. I bet a good looking boy like you makes all the girl's hearts flutter.' Her comment made me blush even more. I looked at her and for the first time ever I noticed flecks of grey in the auburn hair. Her face although immaculately made up, couldn't hide the lines of age. I realised then that Mrs Rowntree was ageing.

'Can I help you with something?' I asked calmly.

'I came to say goodbye Sam and to give you this,' she held out a brown sealed envelope. 'It's just a little something to thank you for all your attention you have given me, not to mention the help with plants.'

'I...oh...you're leaving?' I asked lamely as I took the envelope off her.

'Yes, we are moving to London. Alec has been promoted to head office,' she smiled. I knew that, whatever her age, Mrs Rowntree's face would always light up whenever she smiled.

'I'll miss you.' I said impulsively.

She put her head back and laughed. 'I'm not so sure about that. You will be too busy with whoever you were thinking about just then.'

'No I won't!' I said adamantly. 'I...I can't!'

Suddenly feeling the need to talk about my feelings and my fears. I blurted out all about the happenings of that morning. Finding out about Ede and Tom Lister, how my Dad felt about the Lister family and about my own feelings for Phyllis.

'Does she feel the same?' Mrs Rowntree asked gently taking my hand.

'What, oh, no I don't...I mean I haven't...'

'I know you wouldn't do anything untoward young Sam,' she gave me another glorious smile.

'I'm sorry, I shouldn't be speaking to you like this. It will all sort itself out.' I gabbled.

'I'm sure it will Sam, one way or another. Just promise me this, if you do fall in love with this girl don't fight it. You will regret it for the rest of your life. Tell your Ede the same too.' Her voice sounded distant and I could see she was miles away. 'I know only too well, no you mustn't fight it young Sam no matter how you may think your family feel about this girl.' She leaned forward and kissed me on the cheek. 'Goodbye young Sam, good luck and be happy.'

As she turned I saw her brush a tear from her cheek, I knew it wasn't because she was leaving me, it was because of what she had just been saying about loving someone.

'Bye...' I called, but she had already gone out of my life, I knew I would never see her again and it was my turn to brush a tear from my eye.

Opening the envelope I found five ten pound notes tucked inside a sheet of blue Basildon Bond Writing Paper. On it Mrs Rowntree thanked me for all my hard work and signed it, fondest wishes Helena Rowntree. I kept that note for years, maybe still have it somewhere. As for the money well I knew there and then where that was going, a refrigerator. Yes, I would buy Mam a refrigerator. For a few minutes I forgot about Ede, Tom, Dad and even Phyllis. I held the sheet of paper to my nose and breathed in the familiar smell of the perfume Helena Rowntree always wore. I would miss her, Helena Rowntree was a lady in every sense of the word, and even though it wasn't my place, I wished I'd got to know her better.

Hazel Stevens

7 - Full House

Mam stayed down in London for a few more days and returned with the twins and a rather disgruntled Conway. Dad glowered at them and they stared up at him wide eyed. The twins cried 'Dada,' when they saw him, Mam laughed and Dad told them firmly he wasn't their Dad. Though we all smiled, as the older Ike got the more he looked like Dad. Mam explained that for time being, the younger children would be living with us. It seemed Ike was going to leave London and come back to Leeds to live, either with or without Lily. Frankie was at a nursery school, Ike had arranged with a neighbour to take him and pick him up. Until Ike could find work back home they would be staying in London. Dad snorted as Mam told us Ike was hoping to find Lily and persuade her to come back to him and the kids.

'They're better off without her.' Dad told us.

'Oh Alf, how can you say that?' Mam protested, 'She is their mother.' Mam protectively clutched Shirley and Buddy to her one on each knee. As if sensing insecurity Conway wrapped himself round my feet. Just why he had taken to me quite so much I don't know. In most ways Conway was a miniature Ike. The other three seemed to resemble Lily. Thin, pale and sulky. I hauled Conway on to my knee and bounced him up and down. The little lad chortled with glee. Shirley began to bounce on Mam's knee and she smiled hesitantly. Buddy began to whimper.

'Sam, give Conway to yer Dad and can you go to chippy? I don't feel much like cooking tonight.' Mam sighed wearily and I could see her trip to London had taken its toil. Looking after three small kids was the last thing Mam needed.

'Where's Ede?' She asked. Dad and I exchanged furtive glances. Mam was too quick for us.

'What's been going on?' She demanded.

I ducked into the kitchen muttering I'd go for tea. Leaving Dad to explain how we had hardly seen Ede since last Saturday.

Ede had sheepishly come home that Saturday tea-time, when she knew I'd be in from work. On Sunday she stayed in her room saying something about home-work. Only appearing downstairs for her meals. Dad and her didn't speak. I tried to make conversation but it was all becoming so awkward. I was most relieved Mam came home on the Wednesday.

On my way to the chippy I met Ede in the alley, and knew by her glowing excited face she had been with Tom Lister. I caught her wrist, 'Ede he hasn't, you wouldn't?' I asked cautiously.

'What do you think I am?' She gasped, the happy glow fading to angry disbelief. She shook herself free and turned towards home.

'Mam's home.' I told her. Ede's face spread with a large smile, she pushed past me and ran up the alley.

I got on my bike and pedalled slowly down the alley. Mam had enough on her plate without acting as peacemaker between Dad and Ede. I knew Dad would never change his mind about Farnley Hills and Ede would just have to accept that.

On my return I closed the back gate quietly and leant my bike against the yard wall. Taking off the bag holding the steaming fish and chips, I cringed as I heard the woeful young cries of the twins. Mam was in the kitchen holding Conway on her hip and setting the table with her free hand.

'Where's Our Ede?' I asked her.

'Upstairs,' Mam shrugged.

'Well she should be helping you.' I gasped pushing past my startled Mam and dropping the bag containing our tea on the table. I heard Mam sigh behind me as I strode to the stairs. Taking them two at a time I flung open Ede's bedroom door. She was sobbing into her pillow. Before I could speak she flung herself into my arms.

'Sam, Sam,' she cried. 'Mam asked him again and he still said no. So I told them. Dad had a right go at me and at our Mam. I...I couldn't bear it.' She broke down in tears again. I grabbed her by both shoulders and shook her. She stared at me in astonishment. Sitting her firmly down on the bed. I asked her when she was going to stop being so selfish. Not giving her chance to retaliate I blazed on about Mam, Ike and the Lily situation. How she knew Dad would never change his mind and she had to accept she wasn't going to Farnley Hills. If she didn't want to go to Wharton she could get a job.

'Sam, Sam,' she cried standing up and shaking me.

'I'm not going to Farnley Hills, well not full time anyway.'

'Then, what's all this about?' I stared at her suspiciously.

'I'm getting a job, least I've got a job, I start in the summer.' She finished proudly, sniffing back the tears.

'So what's wrong with you then?' I asked.

'Dad thought I'd be going to the Mill, but I told him I've got a job as an apprentice mechanic at Tom's garage...'

'You what?' I screamed.

'I can work and go to Farnley Hills one day a week. I know it won't be engineering but it's the next best thing. Oh Sam, it will be great working with Tom.' She gabbled on and I sat on the bed watching her.

Mam shouted tea was on the plates and we should go now. I walked wearily down the stairs, dreading what Dad had said about Ede's latest bombshell.

Glancing into the living room I saw the twins sitting on the sofa, a huge cloth covering their knees and they tucked happily into chips. Conway sat at the kitchen table. His face just over the top of it and he too was shovelling chips into his mouth. Dad was nowhere to be seen. Mam looked upset.

'Gone to the pub.' She answered my unspoken question. 'She's told you then?'

I nodded and put an arm round Mam's shoulders. 'Shall I take her tea up?' I asked.

Mam nodded, 'He'll never stand for it Sam,' she said quietly. I nodded and busied myself placing a plate of fish and chips on a tray.

'Leave some for me.' I joked with Conway.

The little boy giggled nervously. He, like the twins, had obviously witnessed Mam and Dad having words and yet they seemed to have taken it all in their stride. Hunger and the delicious chips fading any bad memories. Either that or they were used to disagreements. I did think it was possibly the latter. I knew Mam and Dad wouldn't have argued, I didn't hear any raised voices, so I was glad about that.

In silence I placed Ede's tray on her bed and ignoring her thanks I went back down stairs. I was angry with her for her selfishness and her thoughtlessness. She should be helping Mam with the little uns not causing all this havoc. Would life ever be the same again and what would happen when Ede left school and went to work with Tom? I'd no doubts that she would do just that, she was just as stubborn as our Dad. It was going to be quite a while before life at Number One Congleton Terrace was back to normal if it ever would be. I sat down beside Conway and ruffled his mousy mop of hair.

'Am, Am,' he giggled. Just as Ede had done when she was his age. Sighing and smiling back at him, I inwardly damned Our Ede, for the upset she was causing, and even more so Lily for walking out on her children and our Ike.

In those few days I seemed to grow up such a lot. I suddenly felt a lot older than my nineteen years. Mrs

Rowntree was out of my life. Ike and Lily's separation made me realise that not all marriages were as happy as Mam and Dad's. I suspected from what Mrs Rowntree had said on the day she came to tell me she was leaving Leeds, her marriage wasn't a happy one either.

What with Our Ede growing up too, and although still only fifteen, it seemed she had a boyfriend and soon she would be leaving school and starting work. Mam needed someone to help with the responsibility of the little uns and I knew Ede wasn't having anything to do with them. Her head being so full of her plans, it seemed everyone else could go and whistle.

'I'll bath Conway and Buddy Mam if you like.' I said. Shirley had fallen asleep on the sofa cushions. Her rosebud mouth in half a smile. Asleep she looked like Mam, but when she opened her eyes it was Lily's large mournful eyes staring up at us.

'They can all be wedged in Ike's bed,' she said. 'I'll sleep in yours.'

I shook my head and told her I would sleep in my own bed, she looked like she needed a good nights sleep.

'Thanks Sam,' she nodded wearily. 'You're a good lad.'

I took my charges upstairs, carrying both wriggling boys. Running the water into the bath, I stripped Conway and he splashed about happily while I undressed Buddy. I had to hold him in the water and at first he protested loudly then copied his brother splashing the water.

Ede came into the bathroom, 'Need any help?' She

asked.

I nodded, but couldn't bring myself to speak. I turned my back on her and splashed water at the two little boys. Ede perched on the side of the bath.

'I have to do this Sam,' she said flatly.

'Couldn't you have waited?' I asked her scathingly.

'The forms for Farnley have to be in by Friday, I knew Mam would be back,' she smiled smugly. 'It doesn't matter anyway, cos Tom and I knew Dad would say no. So we asked Tom's boss and once he saw how good I am he had no hesitation in agreeing to the apprenticeship. It's great isn't it Sam.'

She looked so happy, I nodded, no one could fall out with Our Ede for long. 'Dad?' I asked, watching her face.

'He'll come round,' she said slowly, her brow creasing in a deep frown.

'Will he?' I asked. 'This is Dad we're talking about.'

Ede might think it was all cut and dried, but I knew different. Dad would not be held to ransom like she thought. To Ede it was all cut and dried, Farnley Hills or a job. I knew it was all far from being over. Our Ede could be so naive sometimes.

She grinned aimlessly at me. 'Seeing as you are managing, I'm off.' She upped and left. Earlier resentment grew, she had just asked if I needed help, yet went off without giving any.

'Typical.' I told the boys, they laughed and splashed water at me.

The next evening, after I'd gone to bed, Dad and Mam started having a discussion. I heard Mam's voice rise a little and I buried my head in my gardening book. It was by a chap called Percy Thrower and what he didn't know about gardening. When I heard voices rise again I sat upright in my bed straining to hear what Mam and Dad were saying. It was muffled. I peered across at the terrible trio, as I had christened them, in case they awoke. Conway shifted restlessly, but didn't wake. I had slept fitfully the previous night as the kids liked a light on. Now I could use this to my advantage and read for as long as I liked.

'Now look here Lib I am not saying any more, I have signed Ede's college forms and that's the end of it. She either goes on the secretarial course at Wharton or into the Mill Offices as a junior. That's it! Do I make myself clear! I shall post these off in the morning.' Dad's voice was loud and adamant. I think he intended his words to be heard upstairs too. As Ede's bedroom was at the end of the long landing I doubted she would hear. I decided to keep my own council and let Mam and Dad sort it out. I would have a word with Ede about the kids though.

Early next morning presented me with the ideal opportunity. The twins woke up crying and Conway was clambering all over me. I focused on my clock, five thirty. Groaning I hushed the three of them and began to sing Baa Baa Black Sheep. Conway grinned, Shirley stared at me and Buddy whimpered. Our Ede opened the bedroom door giggling. She plonked herself down on Ike's bed.

'Oh don't give up on my account. I think Elvis may have a rival.'

I threw my pillow at her. She lay the twins down and tucked them in crooning softly. Conway was given a book to look at and he snuggled down under the covers watching Ede intently.

'Ede, you have the knack. Why don't you do child care?' I asked.

She frowned at me. 'The only kids I will be looking after is me own. That is if I have any.'

'Look Ede it's gonna be hard enough the next few weeks. Our Mam looks fair worn out. We're all gonna have to lend a hand.' I nodded at the three infants who were dozing back to sleep.

Ede nodded and hung her head. The kids had been here two nights and this was the first time she even acknowledged them.

'Mam does look tired,' she agreed solemnly.

I nodded silently and felt glad she had realised. Maybe she wouldn't rock the boat any more. I watched her go towards the door.

'Thanks Sam,' she whispered as she slipped through it. I wasn't quite sure what she was thanking me for. I dived back under my blankets. It was senseless going back to sleep for a hour, so I got my book out. Percy was describing how to deal with greenfly, it made very interesting reading.

'Sam, Sam.' Mam called softly. I opened my eyes

to see my book laying on the covers in front of me. Glancing at the other bed I saw the three children fast asleep. 'Sam it's nearly half past seven I think we have all slept in.' Mam added, nodding towards the sleeping bodies. 'I've never known them sleep so late,' she added with a sigh.

'Must be Our Ede's influence.' I whispered and told her about my sister's intervention earlier that morning. 'She's good with kids Mam, I told her she should do a child care course.'

'If only.' Mam replied with a touch of sadness in her voice. 'Your sister,' she added ruffling my hair. 'Why don't you grow it longer like they all seem to be doing these days?' She asked.

I shrugged at her strange question.

'You're like your Dad. Old school,' she remarked going out of the door. I wasn't sure what she meant. Did she think I was old fashioned? Surely not.

If my Mam thought that, then Phyllis might too. I would grow my hair just a bit longer and next pay day I might get myself some jeans to go out in and not just for work. I lay back thinking of Phyllis and wondered if she would go to the pictures with me. What would it be like? We could walk there holding hands. I would buy her some chocolates and sit with my arm round her in the cinema. Afterwards we could get a bag of chips and I would walk her home. Would I kiss her on the doorstep? No, that wouldn't be proper, not on a first date. I jumped out of bed. What on earth was wrong with me? Day dreaming was for teenage girls. I'd be late for work at this rate. There was enough strife going on without me antagonising things further. The very idea of me going out with a Lister. Dad would have my guts for garters and that would never do. Mam had enough on her plate with the worries about her other son and her daughter. Phyllis Lister would have to remain a fantasy. My mind was firmly made up on that score.

It didn't matter what Mrs Rowntree had said. Yet I thought about the vacant look in her eyes as she said it. I realised that morning she was a sad lady whose head had ruled her heart for whatever reason. She told me not to let that happen but I knew it must though. To keep the peace. I shut Phyllis Lister out of my mind and out of my heart.

Ike would be coming home soon and we would have a very full house, I mused at the thought and wondered where they would all sleep. Even more so how we would all get on and how Mam would manage with this extended family.

Hazel Stevens

8 - Ede Turns Over a New Leaf

The house seemed unduly quiet that evening when I got home from work. Mam was in the kitchen peeling potatoes. I looked at her enquiringly.

'Upstairs, Ede's got them all in the bath.' Mam answered my unspoken question. She smiled at the look of astonishment on my face.

A while later Ede brought three scrubbed children downstairs for their supper and goodnight kiss off Granny. They drank their milk in silence gazing up at my sister with complete respect. Dad came in and stared at us all in disbelief. In the previous days since the arrival of Ike's children he usually came home to mayhem. They held their faces to him for a kiss.

'Story.' Conway demanded pulling Ede's sleeve. She took them off up to bed without another peep.

Mam explained we would be eating later, it seemed she had agreed with Ede, at Ede's suggestion, that the children be fed and got to bed before we sat down.

For the first time in weeks we ate a normal meal, chatting about the days events. Ede, however, kept unusually quiet.

'Mam, I just have to go to Lucy's to borrow a homework book.' Ede announced at the end of the meal. 'Is it okay if I stay and do my homework with her?'

Mam and Dad exchanged glances and both nodded. She jumped up from the table and grabbed her coat from the back of the kitchen door. 'I'll be back by ten,' she said cheerily her hand on the door knob.

'Don't forget your homework,' Dad reminded her, nodding towards the bag hung up behind the back door.

'Oh yeh,' she blushed. 'Silly me,' she added as she snatched it off the hook.

I frowned at her and tried to catch her eye. She wouldn't be going to meet Tom Lister. No, she wouldn't, Ede wouldn't be so underhand would she?

'Sam, Sam.' Mam called shaking my shoulder, later that evening. I was miles away, staring at a page in my gardening magazine with unseeing eyes.

Looking up I smiled at her and when I saw her tired eyes my smile faded into a frown. Her smooth peachy skin seemed etched with worry lines. I knew the weeks since Christmas Day were taking their toll, so was looking after Ike's three young children. Now Ede was helping hopefully that situation would ease for her. 'It's bedtime,' she whispered.

'Yes Mam, I'll just make a drink. Where's Dad?'

'He went up half an hour since.'

I nodded remembering the television being switched off and Dad calling goodnight.

'Would you like a drink Mam?' I asked as I filled the kettle.

'No I'll just make sure Ede is in and then I'll be straight to bed,' she sighed. I glanced up at the kitchen clock. The big hand just reached the two. Ede was ten minutes late. I gave my own silent sigh of relief as I heard the back gate go. Ede burst into the house. Her young face glowed with happiness.

'You forget your homework?' I asked nodding to her empty hands. She flushed lightly and told me she must have left it at Lucy's. Giving me a smug grin she went through and gave our Mam a big hug and kiss, practically skipping, she carried on through the door and upstairs to bed. Mam and I just looked at each other.

'Sure you don't want a drink Mam?' I asked

'No thanks son, I'll go up,' she smiled. 'You're a good lad Sam.' For some reason I couldn't look at her, I felt choked with tears, so I turned quickly and as the kettle boiled, I heard her follow Ede up to bed.

Inwardly I cursed for the worry caused to my mother by my wayward sister and Ike's uncaring wife. Another night had gone by and Ike hadn't phoned. He hadn't even rung to ask if Mam had got back home with his children.

For the next couple of weeks life at home did seem a lot easier. Ede was helping with the children. She was also keeping her head down. Though every other night she tripped off after tea to do homework with Lucy and she still went to the garage on Saturdays.

Dad signed the forms for Wharton and took them into Ede's school himself. She had mumbled her embarrassment at this but kept quiet in front of Dad. Dad smiled smugly thinking the battle over Ede's future had been won by him. Mam and I exchanged knowing glances but never spoke about it. Mam had enough on her plate. As each day went by and Ike didn't phone she became more and more distressed and worried about her eldest son.

Three weeks after she arrived home with the children and still no word from Ike, Mam announced that at the weekend someone would have to go to London and see what was going on. She stared beseechingly at Dad and me. To my relief Dad told her he would go on Saturday. My sigh of relief must have been audible as they both turned and looked at me. I was afraid they were going to ask me. I just couldn't think of it going to our capital city with its multitude of people, traffic and smoggy streets.

To add extra coal onto an already blazing inferno of worry and concern, Ede didn't come home that night, till nearly eleven. The following hour was fraught with raised angry voices and crying children. Eventually all quietened down with Ede promising never to be late again. Ike's three restlessly crying themselves back to sleep. The house regained peace once more, but for how long?

Satisfied they were settled, I went downstairs to make some cocoa and came to the decision that I must rein Ede in. But how? I didn't want her causing any more rows at home. Nor did I want Mam involved in it anyway. I decided to call at the garage on Friday afternoon on my way home from work. If I got away from the nursery promptly, the place would still be open and I could catch Tom and hopefully Ede would be there too. Yes, I would confront Tom and Our Ede and try to get her to agree to at least give Wharton College a try.

Maybe get Tom Lister to back me up. If I could get that sorted out before Dad went to London, it would be a huge bonus. After all these days many garages had female office workers. She could easily do that. I went to bed that night convinced I could do it. When I closed my eyes it wasn't our Ede I was thinking of as I drifted off to sleep. It was the same face I saw when I was staring at my magazine, miles away. The face of Phyllis Lister filled my head. Her shining golden hair, her large blue eyes and angelic face. Try as I might Phyllis refused to go from my mind and she must stay there all night for she was the first person I thought about in the morning as I awoke.

Throughout February although the days lengthened we still finished early, starting the following month in March we would working later to compensate for winter's short days. Throughout winter I didn't mind the cycle home, seeing the welcoming lights coming on. Thinking about the crackling fire Mam would have going.

The garage doors looked closed as I peddled towards them that Friday evening. I was sure the place stayed open till five or five thirty. As I drew closer I saw a shaft of light spilling from the inside of the workshop. The doors had been left open about five or six inches. Leaning my bike against the wall I peered through the gap, taking hold of the door handle I slid the door back. On well oiled runners it slid smoothly and silently. The dim interior of the workshop and the smell of oil made me glad I didn't work there. An old fashioned black Ford stood over a pit. Beyond it stood a red sports car with the hood up. Low voices met my ears and I strained to hear. Sure enough there came Ede's soft girlish giggle from inside the sports car.

'Ede.' I called, my voice reverberating around the workshop. I stood and stared at the red car. The voices were silenced by my call, very slowly both doors of the car opened and my sister crept out of the passenger side. Her young face flushed with excitement. Her school clothes creased and dishevelled. Tom Lister folded his body out of the drivers side, he hurried round the car as I took a step towards my sister. Tom placed a protective arm around her, his look dared me to go any further. She glanced up at him and smiled at his caring gesture. I stared first at her then at him. They both stared back in guilty silence. Ede's expression a mixture of delight and fear. I stared back at her and suddenly the realisation that they had been doing more than talking spread over me like an icy shower. My face burned and as I stared at her I knew my sister was no longer a girl, she was a woman. Her hand strayed to her skirt and she smoothed it over the creased material. An action she thought might just hide the fact that she had just let Tom Lister make love to her.

I spun on my heel. I felt sick. My head whirled. How could she? How could he? I needed time to think. Time to decide how I was going to deal with this.

'Ede it's time you were home.' I growled over my shoulder as I grabbed my bike.

The cool night air hit my face as I peddled faster. Surely I was wrong. They wouldn't. She wouldn't. You just didn't do that before you were married. I knew I wouldn't. I also knew several lads and lasses who did though and they bragged about it later. I could hear Tom Lister boasting to his mates in the pub on Saturday night. My stomach heaved. Our Ede was disgusting letting him do that. She was as bad as...as our Ike. Yes, he and Lily had slept together before they were married and Frankie was the result.

'Oh God.' I moaned to myself, 'What if...?' No I mustn't think like that. Surely Tom Lister would be more careful than our Ike had been. Tears of anger and frustration filled my eyes. I rammed on the brakes sharply at the other end of Congleton Terrace staring back from the direction I'd just come. Uneasily I stared down the short street to number one. I knew I would have to wait for her. Have to have it out with her now, today.

I waited patiently at the end of our alley, shrugging off conversations with Sid and Joe. They frowned at me curiously, before they went up the alley home. I held my watch up to the street lamp and saw already it was nearly half past five. Dad would be home in a matter of minutes. Ede had to be on her way soon. I went over in my head what Dad might say and what I was going to say to her. I knew Dad would wipe the floor with her. He might even throw her out. I could never be so harsh, but she had to realise what she had just done was immoral. In fact Tom Lister could be jailed for it.

I remembered hearing Sid say half the girls out on a Saturday night were 'jail bait'. I thought he meant too young to be out drinking. Joe enlightened me that Sid meant they were under sixteen and too young to sleep with. I could use this tack on Ede. It was sure to scare her into realising the trouble Tom Lister could be in.

Ede came round the corner into the alley. Her face seemed to glow when she came into the light from the street lamp. She was humming softly. I swung my bike round to bar her way. Seeing me she stood tall and gave me a bold defiant stare. I let my bike drop to the floor as anger engulfed me. I leapt towards her grabbing her by both arms and thrust her back against the wall. She gave a stifled scream and I could feel her trembling. Fear filled her eyes.

'S...Sam,' she cried. 'You're hurting me.'

I felt like shaking her, I held her silently trying to control the rage inside me. At my silence the look of fear on Ede's face turned to one of scorn and defiance.

'What the hell do you think you're doing?' She screamed at me, her voice seething with anger.

'What the hell have you been doing?' I hissed at her.

'None of your bloody business.'

'That's where you're wrong!' I kept my firm hold on her arms while I repeated my knowledge of jail bait. 'Lister could be in serious trouble with the police.' I growled tightening my grip. 'Besides you'll get yersel' pregnant!'

Ede's large eyes filled with tears and her face

turned ashen. She winced and leaned her body towards me. I dropped my vice like grip and went to put my arms about her. She slipped under my arm and skipped over my bike out of my reach.

'Mind yer own bloody business Sam Wagstaff!' She screeched. I glanced round feeling sure the whole street heard.

'Ede, our Mam has enough on her plate!' I yelled down the alley at her retreating back.

Ede stopped and turned, she opened her mouth to give me another fiery rebuke then changed her mind. I knew I had got to her.

'Sam,' she said softly, 'do you think I am totally stupid?' She fumbled in her pocket and threw a small square packet at me. 'You know what that is?' She asked, as I caught the unopened condom in one hand. Ede grinned. 'Hang onto it Sam, it might come in useful for you and Phyllis.' She threw back her head and laughed loudly.

'You disgust me.' I said throwing the condom back at her forcefully. 'You're no better than the prostitutes who hang around outside the Unicorn.' I picked my bike up and wheeled it towards her. Coming level with her I turned and with a free hand pushed her roughly against the wall.

'Oh Sam don't be such a prude,' she gasped. 'It's wonderful, glorious.'

'Ede, shut up. You should be married before you do that!'

'Well, who says so? Besides Tom and I love each

other and when you love each other it's the most natural thing in the world.'

'Can you hear yourself?!' I stared at her horrified. 'You sound like a whore!' I strode off up the alley after her. I didn't want to even look at her I felt so sick. I couldn't believe how brazen and how common my sister sounded. I was filled with disgust and loathing for her. At that precise moment I knew I'd swing for her if she brought her torrid affair with Tom Lister to number One Congleton Terrace.

I slammed open the back gate and thrust my bike under the lean to. Groping in my coat pocket I took out a hanky and wiped my face. I still felt sick. I jumped as the back door opened and I looked up to see my Dad standing on the top step.

'You okay son?' he asked as the light from the kitchen lit up my face. 'You look like you've seen a ghost.' Ede had her arm through his and stared boldly at me.

'I don't feel too good Dad.' I whispered. At this Ede grinned smugly.

'You've not had an accident.' Dad glanced quickly towards my bike.

I shook my head and told him I felt sick.

'Get yerself inside and Mam'll make you a cuppa,' he held the back door open.

I stepped into the kitchen and looked from Dad to Mam willing my threatening tears to subside. 'I need the bathroom.' I gabbled and fled upstairs to the bolt hole. I quickly rammed home the lock on the door before turning and emptying my stomach down the toilet.

I knelt with my head over it, wondering what was going to happen to my sister. As I retched till I could retch no more I saw a glimmer of hope. Maybe, just maybe, now Tom Lister had made Ede one of his conquests he wouldn't want any more to do with her. The hope grew as I convinced myself that's all he wanted her for. By the time Mam tapped urgently on the bathroom door asking if I was okay, I felt a lot better and told her so.

In blissful ignorance I convinced myself that once Tom dumped Ede she would forget all her ideas of being some kind of mechanic and go to Wharton as Dad wished. I washed my face and stared at the grey reflection. 'You never know Lily might even come back to Ike too.' I mouthed to the mirror. A smile spread slowly over my face as my normally ruddy colour returned. Yes everything was going to be okay I concluded as I flushed the toilet and headed downstairs to reassure my parents I was okay.

Ede passed me on the stairs with her three charges, she smiled at me. I turned my face away as I heard her tell the little ones it had to be a quick bedtime story as she was going out.

I could hardly bring myself to look at Our Ede across the tea table. Only a couple of times did I glance across and my stomach heaved a little as I saw the smug expression on her face. My tea stuck in my throat but somehow I forced it down.

'I'm going to Lucy's to do my homework tonight,' she announced as we finished eating. Dad looked up sharply and before he could speak, Mam smiled and nodded telling her that was fine. I noticed Dad grimace and later when Ede left I heard him say to Mam it would have been nice to be asked if she could go.

'I don't know what's got into that girl. But she seems to be getting her head down ready to study at Wharton. She's got the kids well trained with early bedtimes too,' he concluded.

I opened my mouth to tell them Ede had no intention of going there and then closed it again. Dad was going to London the next day and as I said to Ede they had enough on at the moment. Besides Tom Lister would be telling her to get lost. Any minute now she would come home in tears, feigning, no doubt, a row with Lucy. Hopefully she would realise she had just been used.

After tea I took up my usual seat on the sofa, gardening book in hand. However I must have dozed off, yet I could hear Mam's voice telling Dad to leave me and let me sleep. I started dreaming. It was rather vague Ede had got herself pregnant and Dad was shouting at her. It only took seconds for me to hear Dad shouts weren't in my dreams but for real. I stirred and walked to the kitchen doorway. I saw my sister standing in the kitchen staring boldly at Dad. He stared back. For some reason I thought just how much alike they were. Mam was gripping the kitchen table.

'You can't make me. You can't make me.' Ede was shouting at Dad.

'You will do as you are told my girl. Just who do you

think you are?!' He railed back.

'Ede Wagstaff!' She replied cockily. She opened her mouth to add something, but Dad lost it and gave her a swift hard smack across the face.

'Get to your room!' He growled. In shock we all froze and nobody spoke. Mam opened her mouth slowly and reached her hand out towards her daughter. Tears filled her eyes as the gesture was shrugged off. Ede stood staring at Dad completely dry eyed.

'Get out of my sight.' Dad snarled, his head hung forward onto his chest and he didn't raise it until Ede left the room. The silence broken by her hammering footsteps running upstairs.

'Alf, Alf, how could you?' Mam sobbed back the tears, instinctively Dad went to her and placed an arm round her shuddering shoulders. I saw Mam stiffen. I knew her trust had been broken. Dad had never lifted a finger to any of us.

'I'm sorry Lib,' he said softly. 'I should have done it years ago and then she wouldn't be causing all this today.'

'She only wants to do what's in her heart.' Mam gulped and stared up at her husband. 'You know like you wanted to and couldn't.'

'Huh.' Dad grunted and squeezed her shoulder tighter. A look of deep remorse filled his face.

I stared helplessly from one to the other. Without a word I slipped away unnoticed and went to bed myself. Going to the bathroom I could hear the muffled sobs from my sister. Perhaps I should go to her I thought and then remembering the row earlier dismissed this idea. This was all her fault and if she was old enough to decide her own future then she was old enough to accept the consequences of her decisions.

9 - My Decision

Next morning I found Dad had left for London. He'd caught the early train. The twins were still asleep. I went downstairs to find Conway sat on the kitchen floor playing with Mam's pans.

'Is everything okay Mam?' I asked. I'd tossed and turned through the night worrying about it all.

Mam nodded and smiled, her face look quite at ease really. She looked up as the door opened and Ede came through it carrying Shirley.

'Okay love?' Mam asked taking the child from her.

Ede nodded and said, slowly, she would be going to the garage for the day.

'I know Dad's away Mam, but Tom is stripping down his mates E Type Jaguar. I've just got to be there.' Ede gabbled happily as if nothing was wrong.

'You're n...not going there?' I said.

'Mam?' Ede insisted, completely ignoring me.

'Of course you can go there.' Mam laughed, 'Come on little one let's get you dressed and wake your brother up. You too Conway.

The boy stopped banging on the pans and tottered after his Granny.

'You're really going to the garage?' I asked Ede quietly when Mam had gone upstairs.

'Yes and just why shouldn't I?' She hissed back at me.

'I just thought you and L...Lister were f...finished.'

101

I stammered out.

Ede put her head back and laughed. 'Oh don't tell me please Samuel Wagstaff you're just like the rest, get what you want and leave.'

I stared at her and opened my mouth to deny her accusations but the words wouldn't come.

'Sorry to disappoint you brother dear,' she smirked, 'but Tom loves me.' Grabbing a slice of toast and her coat she marched out slamming the back door triumphantly behind her. I stared at the door speechless. Cursing myself for my stupid naivety.

Mam reappeared about ten minutes later a child in each arm and Conway paddling behind her. I took Buddy from her and he giggled with glee.

'Sorry mate I have to go to work. Mam will you be okay on your own with these three?' I asked.

'Of course I will, how do you think I manage the rest of the week, you get yourself off to work. I guess Ede has gone?' Mam spooned cereal into three bowls.

Buddy started pulling my hair. I winced.

'Come here you little devil.' Mam laughed, 'Our Sam'll have no hair left, he'll end up like your Great Granddad!' Mam and I started laughing as we remembered her Dad's shiny bald head, which had to be smothered in sun cream in the summer. He refused to wear a hat and always suffered from a sunburnt head.

I picked up my packed lunch and saw one made up for Ede. Mam had done one as if she had been expecting Ede's request.

'I'll drop this in Mam.' I said quickly.

'No, no,' she said, 'it's okay I will take it round. The kids will enjoy a walk.' She said firmly.

'No Mam don't worry I'll go.' I said, picking up the box and closing my eyes. The scenes of the previous evening swam before my eyes. I couldn't let Mam be met with something similar. She took the box from me and assured me she would go. Reluctantly I let go, searching for something to say. I looked at Mam and her three little charges. Sighing deeply and praying Lister and my sister were behaving themselves, I took myself off to work.

The day dragged despite being busy. Occasionally I would imagine I saw Mrs Rowntree walking round the plants, then I remembered she had moved. I missed her, I felt that day she was the only one I could confide in and she would know what to do. Lister would be at our local pub that night. A crowd of them always met up there on Saturdays before taking themselves off into Leeds City Centre. Quite what they found to do differently in the centre was beyond me. From hearing Ike talk they just seemed to drift from one pub to another. That was stupid when they could stay locally and still have a drink. One pub was just the same as any other.

With a somewhat shaky resolve I felt better. I decided there and then I would see Lister that evening and make everything okay. He was an adult, he would realise what he was doing was wrong, and once I told him Ede was planning a long term future with him. Well, it was bound to frighten him off.

My thoughts then turned to Dad and his trip to London, perhaps he would bring Ike home. Maybe Ike and Lily were back together. That would be fine, the kids would go home and all would return to normal at number one, Congleton Terrace.

I went to our local that night to have it out with Tom Lister, tell him to leave my sister alone, finish it or I would go to the police. Those were my thoughts as I walked boldly up to the bar and ordered half a shandy.

'My God, look what the wind has blown in.' Joe's brother Sid clapped me on the back causing me to spill some of my drink. He laughed loudly. 'To what do we owe the honour of your presence in here?'

I shook my head looking for the right words. 'Just wanted to see what the attraction is.' I said slowly, looking round for Tom Lister.

'Eyeing up the talent too?' Sid grinned. 'Look I can't stop and talk now, got to meet the lads up at the Exchange. Say why don't you come you'll have a grand night in there,' he added saucily.

I shook my head. 'No Sid this is more than enough for me.' I gulped down the shandy it's bubbles catching the back of my throat. I made a hasty retreat. I knew it was no good hanging round for Tom Lister he had obviously gone to the Exchange. No way would I ever set foot in that place. Joe had told me they had strippers performing on Saturday nights.

My meeting with Tom Lister would have to wait. I would beg a dental appointment on Monday and leave work early. That way I could get to the garage before Ede and speak to him then. Later when I heard Ike was coming home I did think of telling him, he would certainly sort Tom Lister out once and for all.

Thinking back now I can't believe how naive I was. How much I wanted for the world to be black and white. With no grey areas. Or was it I just wanted everyone to be happy. I guess it could be the latter as through my life I have worked hard to achieve happiness. That's another story though. That day I felt convinced I could set the world to rights, perhaps it was my own innocent naivety.

Hazel Stevens

Part Two

Hazel Stevens

1 - Determination

I left the house grinning smugly to myself and ran all the way to the garage. Tom looked up sharply as I bounded into the workshop, my face felt pink with the exertion of running. My small neatly rounded chest gently heaving up and down as I caught my breath. He wiped his hands down his overalls and opened his arms. In an instant I was in them and my face was covered with kisses, until his lips reached my mouth. He tasted oily, not that I minded that. I returned his kiss as he had taught me, I wanted him.

The first time we had made love it had hurt and I had cried, after that Tom had been loving and gentle and I experienced sensations I couldn't have dreamt of.

'I want you Tom.' I breathed huskily.

'Later my sweet Ede,' he mumbled into my hair, pushing me away gently he nodded towards the long sleek sports car standing over the workshop pit. 'Work to do.'

'Wow!' I gasped, reaching out running a hand over the gleaming red body of the sports car. 'It's beautiful.'

'Almost as beautiful as you.' Tom grinned, 'Wait till you see what she is like under the bonnet.'

Quickly I rushed round to the front of the car where the bonnet was already raised and stared speechless at the valves and pipes making up the finely tuned engine. Seeing my interest Tom gave me a guided tour of the mechanics. He had soon learnt that you only needed to show me once how something worked and I could grasp the concept immediately. Tom often told me that never in his wildest dreams, did he ever imagine he would meet a girl who shared his deep love of anything mechanical. I could sense him watching me as my eyes examined each working part of the engine. When I turned to look at him, I could see the respect and admiration he had for me. I leant over and kissed him again.

'Best get on then.' I laughed, 'You listening, we ain't time for you to stand there looking all doe eyed at me.' Picking up an oily rag I threw it at him, which hit him in the face leaving a black smudge on his nose, as it dropped to the floor.

'Why you cheeky madam,' he giggled. 'Just wait till later.'

I wiped the smudge off with my hand, he caught hold of it.

'Ede...' Tom's voice trailed off. He seemed to struggle with what he wanted to say to me. 'Best get on.' He let my hand drop, turning abruptly he picked up some tools and began working under the bonnet.

It didn't take long before we both became completely immersed in the work. Apart from the old radio beating out the most popular tunes of the time and the occasional clunk of metal on metal as we worked with the tools, we were silent.

I couldn't help glancing up at Tom now and then. He was the perfect boyfriend and I knew I was deeply in love with him. He filled every waking moment of my life and sometimes every sleeping moment or at least some nights that's what it felt like. Lucy had told me it was just a crush. My best friend had been appalled when I told her I was thinking about sleeping with him. I didn't tell her I had already done so, twice. I knew Lucy would be horrified. Lucy, like Sam, believed that sex was something you had to do when you were married. She had almost made me promise not to do it. I kept my fingers crossed when I agreed, I believed this would render the promise void. Besides now I had done it. Oh how I longed to tell her how wonderful it was, well after the first time. Besides I was going to marry Tom Lister, so it didn't matter if we were having sex before then.

Lucy and I had grown up together, but that seemed to be all we had in common. We were as different as chalk and cheese, but they do say opposites attract, so I guess that's why we stayed friends. Though she didn't like me being pals with Sadie, she didn't know or rather I didn't tell her when I made arrangements with Sadie for us to do something together. Working at the garage on Saturdays gave me an excuse not to go with Lucy on her shopping trips to buy girly clothes. Who wanted that? Certainly not me!

Shortly before lunch time Mam stepped into the garage with three startled children gazing round them in wonder. Conway greeted me with a huge chortle and flung himself at my greasy overalls.

'Mam, what you doing here?' I gasped, bending

down to tickle the twins wriggling about in their push-chair.

'Forgot your lunch.' Mam held out the wrapped sandwiches. 'Where is everyone?'

'Well the owner doesn't come in on Saturdays and Tom, he's the mechanic, has just gone off for some spares.' I announced with a flourish, glad Tom wasn't there.

'Is this what you really want to do Ede?' Mam asked looking round the grim interior.

I nodded eagerly.

'He'll never agree,' Mam said flatly, 'and I'm not sure if I understand either.' She added grabbing Conway as he was about to pick up a very greasy spanner.

Mam left, leaving me to sigh with relief. My mother must see now how well respected and capable I was, else Tom wouldn't have left me on my own. I felt sure Elizabeth Wagstaff would be able to talk my Dad round and let me live my dream.

Tom returned with the parts. I decided not to tell him my mother had paid a visit. We resumed work on the sports car. Just finishing as it's owner walked through the doors. I hid my amusement when I saw him. I imagined a young, very tall, bronzed Adonis. Instead Rob Jeffreys turned out to be about fifty, small, fat with a bald head. He nodded his thanks and drove slowly out of the garage and down the road.

Tom pulled the workshop door closed and locked it from the inside. I followed him into the back and watched as he pulled off his overalls. He scrubbed his hands and arms at the sink and plopped down into the one comfy arm chair. I knew he was studying me as I washed. When I finished we reached for our sandwiches. Tom patted his lap. I sat on his knees, wriggling to get comfortable. I took a sandwich and ate ravenously on it.

'Didn't you have any breakfast?' He demanded.

I grinned back and told him I had been working hard.

'OK, yes you have and a good job too, did you hear her when he started her up? You got those spark plugs just right.' Tom shuffled in the chair and I could feel him being turned on. I finished eating and turned to kiss him.

'Not here though, not again. I want to take you somewhere special,' he breathed. 'Right, young miss where would you like to go this afternoon?'

'Err, oh I thought we could stay here.' I said hesitantly not wishing to sound as forward as it sounded.

'Well I would like to take you out. It's a beautiful day and we ought to get out in the country or something.' Tom smiled, he knew what I was suggesting. He had been relieved when I liked it the second time. It had worried him immensely after the way I cried the first. He told me he thought he would never see me again. Last night though, even in the garage, it had been good, I was more relaxed.

'Well I am happy to oblige but where?'

The rest of that bright sunny day passed all too quickly. Tom and I drove, in the garage's battered old van, out towards Kirkstall Abbey and beyond. Early born lambs frolicked in the fresh green fields. Tom parked beside a stream and we climbed a stile and followed the gurgling waters. The grass felt soft under my feet. 'Where are we going?' I asked.

'You'll see.' Tom answered.

After a few more minutes we came upon a stone barn, with a broken door. We squeezed through the rotting timber door and climbed onto the warm dry hay stored in there.

'Thought this might be warmer than the wet grass.' Tom whispered, taking my hand to guide me further into the barn.

'Have you brought all your girl friends here then.' I mocked him. Tom shook his head and explained I was the very first. I didn't believe him so he went on to explain how he had come fishing last summer and found this place when the heavens opened and he needed shelter.

'I suppose I shall have to believe you then!' I said, standing over him as he laid down on the dried grass. 'It smells wonderful.' I added and collapsed down beside him.

'So do you.' Tom sighed and taking me in his arms he caressed my body until I moaned with pleasure.

'Tom...'

'Mmm.'

'What's it like without that on?' My voice shook as I watched him open the condom. I felt very curious as with the condom, I was sure it felt different.

114

'Unsafe, you idiot, unless you want to get pregnant!' He said sharply staring down at me.

Feeling embarrassed, I blushed and reached for him and for the next few hours we were lost in each other, reaching heights of ecstasy I had never felt before. When it was over Tom rolled onto his back and stared up at the cobwebby roof, the light filtered through the cracks in the slates. Even with the birds singing outside it didn't seem the right place. He twisted his head and saw me watching him.

'Ede...' he began. He frowned unable to say the words he wanted.

'Tom?' I felt alarmed, 'You don't want to finish it... you know like s...some lads. Get it and then...You know what I mean? It's just Sam said...'

Tom leaned over and kissed me on my head. He laughed. 'How could you think that my darling girl? What has your Sam been filling your head with now?'

I relaxed and stared up at the roof, 'Nothing really. Look Tom.' I whispered pointing up as two small birds hopped around the old beams. One of them had a beak full of hay. We watched the bird, delighted as the little creature worked busily making a nest in the rafters, while the other bird looked on. I envied the pair of birds and their simple uncomplicated lifestyle.

'Time to get you home.' Tom said standing up and zipping up his jeans. He turned while I sorted my clothes out, ignoring my pleas for him to make love to me again. He went to the doorway and waited. I felt sad as I followed turning to take one look at the old barn. It had been a blissful afternoon, we could come here every Saturday. I, however, had the foreboding somehow that I would never see the inside of this place again. Yet I couldn't explain why I felt like that. It was the perfect place, I told Tom.

He looked wistful. 'We'll see,' he said. 'Oh don't look so worried. I'm not like Sam said!'

Tom dropped me off at the other end of Congleton Terrace. I knew I would be seeing him tomorrow and told him I could try and slip away tonight. If I wore some of the make up, Sadie had given me, I could pass for eighteen and maybe go for a drink with him. Tom shook his head.

'Time enough for that, 'sides you can have too much of a good thing. Get yourself away home girl, you'll wear me out,' he kissed me and I felt his longing. If only. 'We have to be careful. What'll your Dad say?' he whispered. 'I have taken away your childhood, I feel so guilty.'

'Dad's away in London. Besides you didn't make me do anything I didn't want to.' I said throwing my arms round him.

'Even so we don't want to rock the boat Ede.'

'But I love you Tom.'

Tom looked at me long and hard, it seemed as if he wanted to say something. 'Steady on young lady,' he said softly.

I stared at him feeling uncertain, maybe Sam had been right. Tears pricked my eyes. I thought he loved me too. Perhaps he didn't. As if realising my concern

Tom pulled me into his arms and stroked my hair. 'I want you to be with me, but we have to be patient.'

I nodded, I remembered the long talk we had days earlier, before the first time. I knew I had to keep our relationship very quiet or Tom could be in very serious trouble. Even though I had consented, it was against the law to have sex with someone under sixteen. Tom hadn't wanted it to go that far, but I wanted to prove to him how much I loved him. In the end he gave in to what I guess were his manly urges, but I hoped it was because he loved me too.

He looked at me and spoke quietly telling me that Sadie had told him it was just a crush I had on him. Sadie said all girls my age think they're in love with someone when really they aren't. He said he could wait, that there would be hell to pay when it did come out about us. So no good adding fuel to a fire letting it come out now.

'I must keep my desires under lock and key. At least until you have left school. By then you will maybe realise it is a crush you have for me. You are going to secretarial college anyway, even though there's a job for you at the garage,' he concluded stroking my hair again. 'Go home my darling,' he whispered huskily.

I climbed out of the car and leant against the wall watching him drive away. I felt tears welling. Why couldn't he just say he loved me. I knew he did. He must love me. He had made love to me three times now. He had been careful and gentle. Of course he loved me. I turned towards Lucy's house, wanting to tell someone about him. I knew though I could tell no one. It was bad enough Sam had guessed what we had been doing. I wished now I had denied it. Sam had been so sure of himself, I just wanted to show him he couldn't boss me about, not now I was a woman. All the same I wished I could tell Lucy, or even Sadie. Sadie would share my excitement, but then Sadie had told Tom it was just a crush. I couldn't make him believe that I really did love him. Damn Sadie! Tom made me promise not to hang round with his sister as she often got drunk and said things about people she wasn't supposed to. No, I couldn't tell her. I shuddered at the thought of Sadie Foster getting drunk and telling the whole world about Tom's affair with me, a school girl. 'Perhaps it is just an affair.' I thought, I dismissed this idea as I knew I would be seeing him the next day and we could spend all Sunday in the barn together. Dad was away, Mam wrapped up with the kids. For the moment life couldn't be more perfect for me — Ede Wagstaff.

2 - Getting Ready for Ike's Return

Sunday dawned crisp and clear a light frost covered the house roofs making them sparkle. Dad, Ike and Frankie were arriving home later that day. Mam had a phone call last night just as we were about to turn in.

I slipped downstairs, I was hoping to be out before Mam was up. No chance. Mam must have been up since the crack of dawn.

'Oh Mam!' I exclaimed as I tiptoed into the kitchen.

'My word you're up early.' Mam stared curiously at me. I flushed. 'I'm glad you're up Ede we have lots to do. Ike's coming home.'

For a second I smiled broadly, excited to be seeing my dearest eldest brother.

'Coming home did you say Mam?' I asked.

'Yes, you're Dad's bringing him and Frankie home to stay.'

'Oh.' I sat down at the table. I wasn't sure how this would affect my plans. Tom and Ike used to be pals. 'I'm m...meeting Lucy at ten.'

'Well, sorry love, there's too much to do here. We need to get the front room sorted for Ike. I need you here to help.'

'All day?' I asked just as Sam appeared through the door. He looked at me sharply.

'Yes, they'll be home about two and we can have a lovely Sunday dinner together...' Mam's voice trailed off and I guessed she was about to say just like the old times. It wouldn't be. There were going to be four young children in the house. I could sense without asking that something was very wrong with Ike.

'Now Ede,' Mam went on. 'I want you to go to Lucy's quick sharp, tell her you can't see her today and ask her Mam if we can borrow her fold up bed.'

I knew I looked relieved at the chance to escape. Till Mam added Sam should go too to help with the bed. He followed me out into the yard.

'You weren't really going to Lucy's were you!' Sam remarked coldly.

'None of your B. business,' I smarted back at him. 'Look Sam, can you get the bed I just need to go...'

'Oh no, you don't!' He grabbed my arm, 'This way,' he pulled me into Lucy's yard and I knew I was beaten. Whatever my plans were that day had to go on hold. Sam ignored my pleas and knocked loudly on my friend's back door.

Soon we were back home with the bed in the front room. It seemed Mam had decided, Ike, Frankie and Conway would sleep in there. Sam would be in my room. Shirley and me would be in Sam's and Buddy would sleep in Mam and Dad's room. I think Sam and I must have pulled the same face as Mam assured us it wouldn't be forever, but we had to get all the rooms sorted out before Dad returned. Ike would want to rest because he wasn't very well, she added. Sam and I looked at each other, but neither of us felt inclined to press the matter further as to what was exactly wrong with Ike.

It was much later that I found out. Frankie had been left with a neighbour and Dad found Ike in a squat smoking cannabis. I was shocked to the core when I overheard this revelation. Squats and drugs were something teenage drop outs and no hopers were into. Not Our Ike, surely not.

Straight after breakfast Mam dished out her orders of what was to go where, including moving a small wardrobe into the front room. We squeezed out the two arm chairs from Mam's best three piece suite and squashed them into the living room.

'I know it's not ideal and Ike may not want the older boys in with him,' she said. 'But we'll just have to play it by ear.'

The mantle clock in the front room chimed twelve and we were nearly sorted. I just had a few things to move out of my room. I tried to complain bitterly at giving up my small domain to share. Mam was firm and told me Sam needed his sleep as he was working outside in the cold all day. Sam agreed and said he had already had several disturbed nights since Mam returned with Ike's young kids.

'Ede start the potatoes.' Mam said.

'But Mam.' I wailed.

'But Mam nothing!' Mam said in exasperation.

'He'll think you've stood him up.' Sam whispered as I went past him into the kitchen. 'That's if he is even there himself.'

'Get Lost.' I said, looking directly at Sam. It was a

shock to see such despise in his eyes. But I'd grown up, I didn't need his approval.

All the same I did wonder if Tom would be waiting for me. If he was, what would he be thinking about me not being there. Perhaps I could slip out. Mam came into the kitchen and busied herself with dinner preparations. I rolled my sleeves up and started peeling potatoes, I knew there would be no slipping out then or even later.

I was really aggravated with Our Sam. He sounded so smug as if he knew it all. When in fact he knew nowt! Nowt about me, or Tom, or what we meant to each other. Well one day I'd show him, I'd show them all. It was bad enough Mam making me stay in without Sam rubbing my nose in it. My eyes flicked frequently to the wall clock. I knew the Listers had their lunch at one thirty. I also knew Tom went for a drink before his meal. Maybe I could catch him on his way back home. I knew he would understand when I explained. At twenty five past one the dinner table had been set. The veg was on cooking merrily. So I asked Mam if I could slip to Lucy's as I'd left some homework there.

'You'll have to go later,' she said glancing to the front door. 'They'll be here soon and I want the family together.'

I looked at my feet a little shame faced. It's not that I didn't want to be here. I wanted to see Ike. It was just I wanted to see Tom more. I couldn't understand these feelings. I adored my older brother and one time I would have stayed up all night to see him. It's just when I think of being with Tom Lister my body feels warm inside. I could call in the garage after school tomorrow. I would have to wait until then to explain.

The front door opened at ten past two. Ike and Frankie shuffled through it followed by Dad. Mam started crying and hugged all three of them. The younger kids squealed at the sight of them and threw themselves round Ike and Frankie, clasping them both anywhere they could, Ike swung Shirley up. The effort made him stagger backwards. I gasped. Sam put out his hand to steady the pair. My two brothers looked at each other knowingly. I felt excluded. The look which passed between them was so intimate. I knew they shared a secret. Ike looked across at me and I could only stare blankly back at him. My dearest, handsome brother stood before me like an older replica of Our Dad. His hair was limp and greasy, his face pale and gaunt. Great dark shadows hung below his eyes, eyes which once held a magnetic fire, now had a haunted sad look in them.

'Sam, Ede take these three and go and find something on TV.' Mam ushered us gently into the living room. 'Ike, Frankie you're to sleep in the front room, Conway too if he won't be too much trouble Ike.' Mam spoke softly.

Ike shook his head. He didn't utter a word to any of us just nodded at our greeting.

'Now then I bet you're all starving. Dinner's nearly ready.' Mam looked round the three of them and finally Mam got to Our Dad and I saw the brief hug she gave him, their eyes meeting and holding. Sam and I looked at each other, a little lost in our own thoughts at the appearance of our brother. We shuffled the three younger children out and sat them down in front of the television.

The television was quite a recent addition to our house. Great Aunt Eliza had had one for what seemed like for ever. Mam said she got it for the Queen's Coronation. She told me all Auntie's neighbours had been invited into her house to watch it. Mam and Dad had gone too. The neighbours were only admitted if they brought a plate of food. The whole occasion turned into quite a party. Something which highly amused Dad, as he said, Great Aunt Eliza didn't do parties.

It wasn't long before Frankie joined us and we concentrated on the film. I'm not sure what it was called, but the trains held the kids interest.

'Dad's gone for a bath.' Frankie announced. The young lad lowered his voice and confidentially told us his Dad stank so much in the car that Granddad had to open the window. I smiled at the three year old's innocent frankness. I knew I would be the last one to find out why Ike was in the state he was in. Surely it wasn't all to do with Lily leaving him. He was better off without her and I would tell him so the first chance I got. Ike was far skinnier than Sam. After he started work at the nurseries, the cycling had caused Sam's puppy fat to drop away. So much so I heard Grandma more than once tell our Mam to make him some suet puddings. Hopefully Mam would make some for Ike. I looked across at Sam and smiled as I watched him tweak Conway's toes in a game of This Little Piggy. My animosity towards him waned slightly until he looked up and scowled at me. I turned away not daring to speak. This was my life and Sam had no right to interfere with it. It would be worse now, Ike was home and no doubt I'd have to put up with his two pennyworth too.

Mam came in and announced dinner was ready. Dad had gone up to tell Ike. We decided not to wait for him and were half way through our meal when Ike came back downstairs. His hair still damp and combed back off his face. It seemed to emphasise his leanness even more.

'I'll get your dinner son.' Mam slid out of her chair and squeezed past me to the oven. I took over feeding Shirley who had begun to whimper having been abandon by her feeder. Mam pressed a plate of roast beef and Yorkshire pudding down in front of Ike.

He stared at it and then back at her. 'I'm not really hungry Mam,' he said, his voice very weak and quiet.

'Try something, eat what you can,' Mam said gently, she looked away and I knew she was close to tears. We finished our meal in silence. We were watching Ike as he pushed the food round on his plate. He took a mouthful and then another.

'It's good to be home,' he said softly, a smile briefly crossing his face. 'I'll sort something out for us very soon.'

'Now you'll not rush into anything. We're all sorted and you stay here as long as you want.' Mam said looking at Sam and I for our support. We nodded as enthusiastically as we could. Ike looked down at his plate, lost once again in his own thoughts.

The rest of the meal passed in silence. Unusual for a Wagstaff Family Gathering. Ike ate little and even the children were quiet and subdued. Mam and I were clearing up when Ike announced he needed to sleep. So at four fifteen he went off to the front room and we didn't see him any more that day. Mam decided not to put the boys in there with him, all the boys would sleep in the spare bed in Sam's room or my room as it was now. Shirley would go in with my parents. I have to confess the reunited brothers went off to sleep quicker than I imagined. Frankie was quiet and seemed reluctant to join in with Conway's demands to play. My last thoughts that night weren't about Tom but about Ike. I couldn't get the haunted look in his eyes out of my head.

I opened my eyes next morning to find Frankie staring back at me from the bed opposite. The little boy looked lost and confused, seeing me awake he sat up.

'I w...want my Dad,' he said dolefully, rubbing his eyes and staring down at Conway and Buddy. The two smaller boys shifted restlessly but didn't wake. I got out of bed and beckoned Frankie. Together we crept downstairs and I quietly opened the front room door. Ike was awake and lay looking up at the ceiling. As he glanced our way he gasped and stared from me to Frankie.

'Ike, what's matter?' I whispered.

'Ede,' he said and turned away. Frankie looked up at me and back to his Dad.

Large tears had welled in the child's face. I put an arm round him but he shrugged it off.

'Dad,' he gulped as the tears fell.

Ike turned and looked blankly at the boy. Slowly it seemed as if he began to recognise Frankie and he spread out his arms. The boy needed no more, he leapt onto the bed and clung onto his Dad sobbing his heart out. Ike hushed him and gently stroked his hair. I felt like an intruder and retreated from the room. My stomach heaved and I had to run up to the bathroom. The process of being sick brought tears to my own eyes. I washed my face and realised I was shaking. I jumped as Dad rattled on the door calling for whoever was in there to hurry up. I heard him retreat back to the front bedroom as Shirley began to cry. Feeling relieved I crept back to my own room and dressed quickly. Just finishing when Buddy woke up and thumped his brother on the chest causing Conway to wake up himself and retaliate until I plucked Buddy from his reach.

'Now Conway, come on your Dad and Frankie are downstairs, lets get dressed...' I tailed off as the delighted Conway leapt out of bed and scrambled down, shouting for his Dad, with all the exuberance of a lively two year old.

Buddy wriggled in my arms and grabbed my hair. I dumped him unceremoniously on the bed and gave him a teddy to play with while I brushed my hair and put it up into the high pony tail. I loved the feel off my long hair swinging to and fro as I walked along. Tom said it made me look cheeky.

Tom, it had been the first time I had thought about him since waking. I sighed as he was usually my very first thought. I picked Buddy up and hugged him close to me.

'Me and Tom are going to have a bundle of kids too when I'm older.' I said and kissed him on the cheek. Buddy giggled and tried to grab my pony tail. 'Oh no you don't you little monster. Breakfast?' I stood up and carried my charge downstairs.

'Well Shirls look who's here.' Mam said as she spoon fed Buddy's twin. 'Would you feed him Ede love?'

I sat down with the wriggling child on my knee, he was eager not to miss out on anything his sister might be getting. Holding him with one hand and pouring milk into a dish with the other I soon placated him and he eagerly wolfed down the soft cereal.

'We shall have to see if we can't get another high chair.' Mam said handing Shirley a slice of thickly cut bread and butter to chew on. The little girl chuckled as she stuffed it into her mouth. The high chair she was in took up quite a lot of room in the kitchen already. Where Mam thought we'd put another one I didn't know. 'Frankie awake? Where's Conway?'

'Yes Mam, they're in with Ike.'

'Oh why did you let them go in there, Ike needs his sleep.' Mam raised her voice.

'But he was awake Mam.' I said in my defence.

'Oh.' Mam stared at the teapot for a moment, lost in her own thoughts.

'Mam what's wrong with Ike?' I began. She didn't answer. 'I mean he must be over Lily by now?' I asked.

'Oh my darling girl,' she said stroking her hand over my hair. 'You will know when you're in love it takes a lot longer than a couple of weeks, to get over someone, as you put it.'

'But I...' I stopped myself. How could I tell her I was in love. I so much wanted to but I knew I mustn't not yet anyway. I would tell her soon. I just wouldn't tell her who it was. Yes I could do that, pretend I had a crush on someone at school. Why I could tell her now. 'Mam...' I broke off as Dad appeared in the kitchen. He had some shaving cream behind his ear. I reached out to wipe it off.

'Say, what are you doing girl?' He snapped. I dropped my hand away.

'Trying to make you look half decent.' Mam laughed and dabbed the cream away with the kitchen towel.

'Oh,' Dad looked at me briefly. I knew the row between us, about which college I wanted to go to, hadn't abated, at least not in his mind. In mine it was immaterial I was going to work with my darling Tom. 'Ike up,' he added tersely.

'I'll go and see.' I needed to get away from him, yet

didn't understand why. I thrust the confused Buddy at Mam and rushed to the front room.

Ike didn't hear me open the door, I stood looking at his thin naked body. He had his back to me. But I could see his vertebrae sticking out and his skin looked withered and wrinkled. He didn't look a bit like Tom. Tom had firm soft skin which covered his muscular frame tautly. I felt like a peeping Tom, as my brother stooped to put on his undies. I pulled the door closed and knocked loudly.

'You up yet, Dad wants to know?' I called.

'What, oh yes.' Ike mumbled. 'Not too much noise our lass, Frankie's gone back to sleep.' He peered round the door at me. His face seemed thinner and whiter than yesterday. His hand trembled as he held the door.

'Ike are you okay?' I was frightened, he looked so ill, I wondered if he was going to die. 'Ike are you okay?' I asked again as he stared blankly at me.

'Yes our lass, yes I am,' he stilled the trembling hand and smiled weakly. 'Now scat let a body get dressed. Can't have you seeing half naked men at your age!' He scoffed lightly and I blushed. My face felt hot, I turned away not wanting him to see. He could always read me could our Ike. 'Ede..?' He began. 'I'll be there in two ticks.' What had he been going to say? I knew I must control myself or he would guess. Maybe Sam would tell him or had he already told him? No, I didn't think this likely. Sam could see Ike had enough problems. Sam would also know Ike would tell my Dad.

I had always been a bit jealous of the closeness Dad and Ike shared, even though they were as different as chalk and cheese. I wondered why Sam didn't feel the same envy, but he assured me he didn't and asked me once why should I. Dad loved all of us the same and if anything he and Ike were jealous of me because I was the youngest and a girl and spoilt. The banter had developed into a sibling argument, which had, I recall made Mam angry with both of us.

I needed to talk to someone about Ike. I needed someone to find out what was wrong with him. I would ask Tom. He and Ike used to be friends. Tom could call and see Ike, ask him out for a drink. Why, Tom could come round to our house often, get to know Mam and Dad, as a friend of Ike's. They would get to like him and when it all came out me and him would be getting married, they would be okay. As they would know him and have already accepted him as Ike's friend. Ike would be thrilled. I would see Tom more as he could come and spend time here with Ike and the kids. Yes it was perfect.

Hazel Stevens

3 - Looking Back

Thinking back to my childhood days, I can't quite remember when I became interested in how things worked. Perhaps it was finding Sam's cars and investigating them. I remember the fascination with the kettle too and of course I had eagerly sat by Ike as he fixed his bicycle, something he always did and he fixed Sam's too. It didn't take me long to work out how to get into the kettle to see how that worked. Mam was upset as I recall. But we seemed to have a special bond. I assumed it was because I was the youngest and also the only girl.

I detested the dresses Mam always wanted me to wear and it didn't take long for me to realise if I got them dirty she would dress me in romper suits and shorts. So in my new pretty dress I would carefully make my way to the coal scuttle and play building blocks with the lumps of coal. Safe in the knowledge Mam would never be cross, she would just sigh and dress me more comfortably.

Ike's motorbike was fascinating, I had never seen one up close and I was eager to see how that worked. I must have been pretty strong to undo all the nuts and bolts holding the engine in. I managed it and was only saved by Joe's brother. I was mighty scared that day, in fact terrified for my life, especially when it broke down. Ike had been blazing but Mam came to my rescue yet again.

The head teacher at my school had been pretty impressed when I fixed his car and had let my Mam and Dad know, he said I had a talent for mechanics and he recommended I go to college to study it. I was thrilled. Dad however had other ideas and was insisting I went to the blessed secretarial college. I didn't want to work in an office. I loathed the idea. How could he force me to do what I didn't want to? Mam was on my side, I knew that but I also knew once Dad made a decision he stuck to it.

Mam always wanted a new house and when they were building some nice modern semis further out of Leeds, she longed to live in one. Dad stood firm and I heard him say he was going to go out of Number One Congleton Terrace feet first. I wasn't sure what that meant. I just knew Mam had said no more about moving.

I am not sure now how I became friends with Sadie Lister. I hated her at the junior school and I remember hitting her when she told me her sister Joan had kissed our Ike. As if he would have anything to do with that family! Dad hated them all, 'Layabout and bad uns,' he said more than once.

I didn't pass my eleven plus as Mam, Dad and Ike hoped I would. Neither Ike nor Sam had either and we all went to the same secondary school. I was proud of that. It was great talking about the same teachers who had been there when Ike was at school and were still there when I went.

When I met up with Sadie at secondary school, we had a few problems as she tried to bully me. She soon realised I would stand up to her and gradually gave up and I began hanging round her group of friends. Sensing I was not going away, they included me in their conversations, which was usually about boys, make up, hair and dances. They could all jive and talked about the weekly dance they went to or 'bop' as it was called.

Living in the next street Sadie and I took to walking home together and on one such walk, I asked what her family did. She only spoke of her brother Tom and about his work in a garage. My ears pricked up. We met by accident during one school holiday at the corner shop. Sadie said she was taking Tom his dinner down to the garage where he worked.

'Can I come?' I pleaded. Sadie nodded and we set off together.

Staring wide eyed at the vast array of tools strewn around and secretly marvelling at all the bits and pieces of car engine carefully placed on the benches and floor of the small garage. How I longed to go in, handle the tools, ask questions, but instead I just hung back shyly inside the doorway.

'Who's this then our lass?' Tom asked in his deep husky voice.

I smiled shyly as Sadie made the introductions, adding that I was really good with stuff. I blushed as she went on to tell Tom about my triumph fixing the head's car and another teacher's bike.

'Really?' Tom looked amused.

Sadie knew he wasn't really listening. 'She really is good with stuff our Tom! Come on Ede lets get out of here!' She grabbed my arm and pulled me into the street.

Glancing back over my shoulder I saw Tom staring after the pair of us. Our eyes met and he smiled, I felt it was really genuine. I shrugged and smiled back.

'By your Tom's a looker.' I told Sadie.

'If you like them rough,' she scoffed. 'I will tell him tonight how good you are at fixing things, cos I swear he didn't bloody believe me.'

'Language Sadie.' I said automatically as swearing was frowned on in our house.

'What!' Sadie laughed and said 'Bloody's in the bible, bloody's in the book and if you don't bloody believe me have a bloody look!'

I was so shocked I started laughing hysterically and soon we were both falling about, clutching at each other for support. 'Oh Sadie, that's a good un.' I managed to gulp out.

I was mightily impressed when Sadie revealed to me that she wanted to drive the buses. She objected strongly, when I said women didn't do that, saying they did in the War. She added women weren't mechanics either, to which I had to say they did that in the War too. Somehow this shared enthusiasm for wanting to enter a man's world cemented our friendship.

Sadie did admit that Joan hadn't kissed Ike, she had just said it to wind me up. 'You was a right little fire cat at junior school.'

'How do you know I still aren't?' I asked.

'I had better warn our Tom then.'

'What you on about Sadie? Warn him — about what?'

'That you're still a little fire cat, well come one Ede I saw the look on your face and you have already said he is a looker. You fancy the socks off him. Don't you? Well, don't you?'

I tried to deny it, but couldn't, yes I did fancy Tom Lister, but he was our Ike's age at least, probably older. I was a school girl there was no way he would look at me. No way on this earth would anyone like Tom Lister look at plain little Ede Wagstaff.

I persuaded Sadie to let me go, a few times, to the garage with her and gradually Tom realised, I think, I was genuinely interested in engines. It wasn't long before I went on my own some Saturdays. It was a wonder he wasn't sick of my questions about cars. Tom took it all in his stride and when he opened the door to me on that Christmas Day, although I had gone to seek solace from Sadie, Tom answering the door and kissing me, well what can I say, the answer to my dreams. I knew he'd been drinking and it probably meant nothing to him. It meant the world to me and it wasn't long before he realised, it meant more to him too than just a Christmas kiss.

Ike was my concern though, I remember when I was little I was so afraid of him. He was so very grown up in my eyes. Tall and broad. He styled his hair in a quiff like the teddy boys did back then. Our Dad was forever telling him to get it cut. Ike chose to ignore him. He also wore long jackets and shoes with pointed toes.

Sam was quite the opposite, he wore sensible clothes and had his hair cut short. He only seemed to care about plants. There was, however, many a time when he and Ike would argue, Ike teased him about plants and girls. Mam would always break up their squabbles and I don't think they ever really fell out.

Lucy once said she didn't know how our Sam stuck it outside all day. Neither did I, especially working with plants, what was interesting about that. You planted seeds, they grew into flowers and then died. Lucy wanted a nice warm office job and was keen to go to Wharton, she couldn't understand why I didn't want the same. How could I possibly think about getting my hands dirty all the time? As I said before it was peculiar why Lucy and I were friends being so totally different from each other.

It was a shock to see Ike when he came home, with Frankie from London. He was as thin as a rake and looked terrible. Yes I did think he was going to die. I daren't voice my fears to any of the family in case it was true.

I blamed that stupid daft Lily he'd gone and married. She was a right old miserable cow. Don't think I saw her smile once, except for that smirky grin she gave me at Christmas when she guessed I had been kissing somebody.

Ike was far better off without her and so were the kids. Oh I didn't mind looking after them, they were fun in a way. Just that I had other things on my mind. Tom Lister being the main one. That and wondering how to persuade Dad to let me do what I wanted. How on earth could I get round him? These were my last thoughts at night and first thoughts on a morning, after I had said Goodnight to Tom and Good Morning too of course. I would gaze out of my bedroom window, imagine Tom doing the same and I would blow a kiss and whisper the words in the direction of his street. It wasn't the same when I had to move into Sam's bedroom, that was at the back of the house and my blown kisses and whispered words couldn't go round corners. It was a lot of daftness really but at the time it was so important to me that I said Good Morning and Goodnight to my darling Tom.

It didn't seem to matter to Dad what I wanted. I must admit it took some talking Mam round to the idea. She had a strange look in her eyes when I declared it was my life and I should be able to do what I wanted! I wonder now if she had some secret longing when she was young and for some reason couldn't fulfil her dream. I must ask her about it before its too late.

My Mam, Elizabeth Wagstaff, I could not begin to imagine what life would be without her. She is the linchpin of the family. Always there for any of us, keeping us calm. Yes, it will be a sad day when we have to say goodbye. I hadn't really thought of that before, to me she would always be there. However since meeting Tom I often thought what I would do if he wasn't there any more, one thought led to another and round to my family, Mam, Dad and Ike. Ike looked so ill and I wondered if he was going to leave us. I didn't like my Dad very much at that time, but he was still my Dad. My big problem was how to get round him, persuade him that doing mechanics was my heart's desire next to Tom Lister of course.

I managed to get away the next morning before school. Mam ran out of milk and would I run to the shop and get some. I was out the house before she changed her mind. I ran all the way to the corner shop it was a small cluttered place that sold just about everything. Mr Patel owned the shop, he wore lovely, long, brightly coloured dresses, as I used to call them. He was pleased when I told him I liked the colours. That morning I paid for the milk and fled. I was out of breath by the time I reached the garage.

Tom had his head under a car bonnet, which he banged his head on as I fell through the door. 'Now then Ede where's the fire?' He asked rubbing his head. 'Shouldn't you be on your way to school?'

I nodded and quickly explained about Ike coming home, getting the milk and having to give up my room.

Tom grinned at my childish prattle. 'Calm down Ede, knowing Ike it won't be for long. He won't put your Mam and Dad out longer than is necessary.'

'That's just it Tom, Ike has changed and he's ill,' my voice cracked as tears threatened.

'Your Ike never had a days illness in his life!' Tom exclaimed. 'What's wrong with him anyway?'

I shrugged and wiped the tears away with the back of my hand. 'I don't know Tom, would you come and see him?'

'Eeh lass I don't know about that, what with yer Dad an' all.'

'You're Ike's pal Tom, surely Dad won't complain about that, please Tom, please.' I begged. He had to agree and then my plan for Dad to get to know him would soon be in action.

'I suppose I could like, but I tell you now yer Dad ain't going to like it.'

I didn't wait any longer, school beckoned and I had to get the milk home. 'See you tonight then Tom, at ours about seven.' I said blowing him a swift kiss.

Would Tom come tonight and why didn't Dad like the Listers? I asked myself frequently, I had a whole day of lessons before I could find out. That day dragged boringly.

I raced home from school to find Mam in a flap, looking after four children had taken its toll. Knowing Tom would be coming round yet not sure of the time I asked Mam if I should get fish and chips for tea. She nodded gratefully, telling me it was a good idea.

'Where's Ike?' I asked after getting plates and cutlery onto the table. I was half afraid she was going to say out or he'd gone back to London.

Mam jerked her head towards the front room. 'In

there, he hasn't appeared all day.'

'Shall I go and see if he wants to go to the chippy?'

'No.' Mam sighed, 'Leave him be, he needs to rest.'

I opened my mouth to ask exactly what was wrong with Ike, but decided not to, instead I took Shirley and Buddy into the living room. We'd moved the TV in there and though the picture wasn't great with the portable aerial. I managed to find them a kiddies programme to watch. Hearing the TV Conway and Frankie soon joined us. I was glad, it would give Mam five minutes peace until I went to the chippy.

'Where do ya think your going?' Sam snarled as he pushed his bike into the yard. I was just pulling my coat on and closing the back door.

'To the chippy! If you must know!' I snapped.

Sam shrugged and moved to one side to let me pass.

'Don't take all day then.'

I ignored him, he could think what he liked. Him. in his perfect little world. Gardening was all he ever thought about. Might do him good to get a girlfriend. Not that that would happen! Unlike Ike who was quite good looking our Sam was just plain ordinary, not very tall. In fact I was nearly as tall as him then. His face was covered in spots. Acne, which Mam said would go, I was glad that it seemed only lads got it. My skin was smooth and clear, I had and still do have rosy cheeks.

I hoped there wasn't a queue at the chippy and my luck was in, I placed my order and stood back. Lucy came in grinning at seeing me.

'Guess what, Mam got a letter today. I'm off to

Wharton,' she announced with a flourish. 'Just for the day like, to see what its like before we start in September, it's next Tuesday, are you going too?'

I shrugged, Mam hadn't said anything. But I guess she had been busy with the kids. The letter would probably be addressed to Dad anyway as he'd signed the forms.

I collected the newspaper wrapped package of fish and chips. Holding them away from me as the grease was coming through the paper already. My stomach rumbled, I felt hungry, yet the smell in the chippy made me feel quite sickly. 'Gotta run Lucy.'

I hurried home praying that Dad hadn't got a letter. I wasn't going to Wharton even for a day. Would there be another row? I told myself to keep calm and not argue if he had received a letter. It would be difficult as in those days I had quite a temper. I would flounce out the house at the first hint of trouble. I couldn't that night, I just had to be there when Tom came to see Ike.

Dad was home by the time I got in with our tea. Mam busied herself getting the chips on plates for the kids. I sat them all down. Sam and Ike came in and we all managed to squeeze round the kitchen table again. It was a crush and I hoped it wouldn't be for long. Part of me wanted Lily to come back and take the kids away leaving Ike with us. But from what I heard Mam and Dad say that wasn't likely to happen.

After eating my stomach felt better, I got up and began to collect the plates.

Dad put his hand on my arm and told me what I

didn't want to hear. 'Ede, I got a letter from Wharton this morning, you're to go next Tuesday to see if you like it there or rather if they'd like you to go there.'

I opened my mouth to reply.

'No good arguing lass, that's where you're going,' he concluded. Reaching for the evening paper he got up and went into the living room.

I turned to look at Mam for support but her eyes begged me not to start a row about it. Ike slapped me on the back and said, 'Well done our Ede.'

Sam grinned smugly. I could tell what he was thinking. It would get me away from Tom Lister. Ha, no chance Sam, my eyes told him.

A loud knock on the back door echoed round the kitchen. My heart raced, could it be Tom? 'I'll get it.' I said scrambling round the table.

Opening the door, my heart fluttering it immediately sank, I found Joe there. He'd come to see Sam.

'That look for me?' Joe asked grinning widely. 'Or were you expecting someone else?'

I stared at him surely, our Sam hadn't told him, had he? I shrugged and let him in. Would Tom come to see Ike, I'd just have to wait and see.

I didn't have to wait too long. Within half hour of Joe knocking on the door came another knock. 'I'll go.' I said quickly trying to disentangle myself from Shirley's arms clenched round my neck.

'Looks like you're tied up.' Dad said, 'I'll go.'

I wanted to shout no, but Shirley hung on and I watched in despair at Dad's disappearing back through the living room door. It wasn't long before I heard his voice. Though I couldn't hear what he said, he was obviously speaking firmly without shouting. The back door slammed shut and my heart sank, Dad didn't need to tell me it was Tom.

'The nerve of that family!' He grumbled. 'It was that lad, you know the oldest Lister. Wanted to see Ike if you like! As if Ike would have owt to do with them!'

'Oh Alf.' Mam sighed, 'Don't you think Ike should be the one to decide?'

'I sent him off with a flea in his ear, told him Ike wasn't seeing anyone.'

Mam sighed again and looked sad.

'Well Lib,' Dad continued his tirade. 'He isn't fit to see anyone is he? Do you think he should see a doctor? Has he been out that room at all today? Other than for his tea and did you see the way he turned it round on his plate. What a waste of money, he hardly ate a thing. He's going to have to get a grip Lib or I'll be having words.'

Mam shook her head and her eyes filled with tears.

'Mam.' I reached out a hand to comfort her. This was more serious than I had realised. I thought Ike was upset and not eating because of Lily, but at that moment I knew there was something seriously wrong with Ike. 'Mam is Ike going to be okay?'

Mam nodded and I disentangled Shirley, took Buddy off Mam and carried them both upstairs to get ready for bed. Plonking them both in the bath together, I could at last turn my thoughts to Tom and I felt tears threatening.

The two children splashed each other and giggled. I suddenly felt very loving towards the twins. I knew if or rather when Tom and I had kids there would be no way I could leave them. I was astounded Lily could do that, leave the four of them and our Ike. She was a bitch. I said it out loud knowing the kids wouldn't understand or at least I hoped they wouldn't. Though they both stopped splashing and turned their faces up to look at me. Instinctively Buddy reached up his hands so I lifted him out the water and dried him quickly. Before taking Shirley out and drying her too. Mam came in with Frankie and Conway and deposited them in the bath together.

She stroked my hair and swept up the twins one in each arm, she asked me to watch the two boys and could I get the pen mark off Conway's face. She laughed as she pointed to the huge line of blue ink down the boys cheek. I nodded, relieved Mam was OK and smiling again.

4 - What to Do Next...

Yes, exactly, what to do next? It was pretty clear Tom wasn't welcome in our home, even as Ike's friend. Perhaps I could persuade Ike to see Tom and bring him back himself, surely Dad wouldn't go mad about that.

'What do you want me to see Tom Lister for?' Ike said sharply the following afternoon when I asked him if he was going out to the pub at the weekend and maybe link up with Tom and the rest of his mates.

'Well, he called last night and wanted to see you. You're mates with him, aren't you?' I stuttered.

'Not really mates.' Ike said wearily. 'He was in the same gang as Sid and me but that's as far as it went. What on earth possessed him to come round here? I bet Dad went loony.' Ike smiled, obviously the thought of our Dad coming face to face with a Lister had amused him.

I shrugged, what else was there to say. 'Just going out for a bit Mam.' I called on my way out the back door. I needed to see Tom, but had wanted to ask Ike first. Tom would know what to do. I'd chewed it over all day at school hardly paying attention to the lessons, resulting in a lunch time detention. Not that I minded, it gave me chance to formulate what to do next. Even as I ran to the garage I had no idea what to say, but yes Tom would know.

Tom Lister had his back to me as I ran round the corner of Finkle Street. The garage was at one end of the next street, Market Street. Though there wasn't a market there now. It had once been a cattle market where livestock was sold. It had disappeared long before the First World War, but the street still kept its name.

Tom jumped as I put my arms round his waist, the padlock he was in the process of attaching to the door fell to the floor. 'Eeh lass you gave me a fright.'

'Got a guilty conscience.' I laughingly ask.

'Yes. If you must know,' he frowned as he replied and lines creased his forehead.

I raised my hand to smooth them out. He took hold of it and spoke softly to me.

'Ede we have to talk, about last night.'

'That was Dad being Dad...' I started to say.

'No it was your Dad, did you know what he said?'

I shook my head, my body started to tremble. 'T... Tom, please don't take any notice. Ike will talk him round...'

I broke off as Tom's grip on my hand tightened. 'You've not told Ike about us have you? Well have you?'

His voice was so angry I couldn't speak. This wasn't the Tom I'd grown to love, why was he being like that, how could he speak to me like that? I was scared, very scared. He pushed me through the garage door inside. I tried to protest and tell him no, of course I hadn't told Ike. But my mouth was dry and the words wouldn't come. He thrust me down into a chair. I rubbed my hand and watched as he strode up and down in front of me. His hands running through his hair.

'Tom...please.' I managed to find my voice but it was shaky and tears filled my eyes. 'Tom I haven't told Ike. Nor would I. But you could be friends with him, he could bring you to the house. It would be okay. Dad would be okay.' I gabbled on and on. Tom just strode up and down.

'Ede,' he spoke at last and knelt down in front of me. 'Ede oh Ede.'

'I love you Tom.'

'No you don't, it's a school girl crush,' at last he smiled.

I shook my head vigorously denying this, before repeating. 'I love you Tom. I leave school soon, perhaps we could get a flat somewhere, be together, I could work at the garage...'

'No!' Tom stared at me now and my heart filled with panic again, why wouldn't he listen to me. It could work. I knew it could.

'You want to finish it?' I asked shakily.

Tom took both my hands in his. He was going to finish it. But he shook his head. 'Ede you're young. You have your whole life ahead of you. I think we should wait and do what your Dad asks.'

I tried to protest but he kissed my words away. That kiss made me think that perhaps he did love me. I asked again was he going to finish with me. He denied it.

'But I think you should keep the peace with your Dad, go to secretarial college.'

It was as though Tom looked at me as a young girl,

I knew he thought it was a crush and I might get over it if I went to secretarial college, he said I would forget all about him. It would be me finishing with him then.

'We have all the time in the world Ede, we can wait. At least your Dad cares about his family which is more than mine does.'

'You don't want to finish with me then?' I asked again, holding my breath waiting for his answer. He didn't reply just looked at me, I started to cry. This was it, this was the end. I couldn't bear it. I curled up in the chair hugging my knees. 'Please Tom don't do this, please I love you.'

I knew some would say have a bit of pride girl, but right then I just wanted Tom to love me.

He pulled me up into his arms and murmured, 'I just asked you to hold on, go to secretarial college for your Dad, keep the peace. Ede I can't say anything else.'

I pushed him away. 'You don't want me any more do you?' Tom grabbed my hands in his. I tried to break free. Why wouldn't he let me go. But he held on. Why, when he didn't love me? Didn't want me!

He pulled me close to him again. Placed his arms round me. 'Oh Ede, I do want you,' he breathed, gently kissing my tears away. 'I want you every day but we must be patient, please Ede.'

I tried to free myself again but Tom held me close, I couldn't understand what he meant. Why would he be telling me to go to Wharton yet say he wanted me every day? I was so confused. Words didn't mean a lot to me in those days. Actions spoke louder than words. 'Love me Tom, make love to me.' I kissed his face finding my way to his lips. I ran my hands over his body and could feel his need against me. He returned my kiss with a deepness, arousing feelings I hadn't really experienced before. He loved me, I felt sure of that. 'Love me Tom.' I said pulling him closer to me.

'I haven't any,' he said sadly.

'Be OK just this once won't it?' I replied naively.

'I suppose.'

We made love and I felt all the love I needed from him. I knew I was under age, jail bait as they said. But I didn't care, I loved Tom and now I knew he loved me.

'I'll never end this Ede. I do want us to be together but we must wait at least until you are older. Please go to secretarial college. We could get our own garage. I'm useless at paperwork but you will learn all that there is to know at Wharton. Do our books and sort out that stuff.'

I nodded. Our own garage he said, that would be perfect, I'd do the paperwork. Yes I could see now how Wharton would help me. 'But what about me learning mechanics?'

'Well you can still come here on a Saturday, I'll ask the boss if he'll give you a Saturday job and in the holidays too. OK it might not be official like, but I can teach you all you need to know, I know you won't get a qualification. But after Wharton, you could go to Farnley Hills. You'll be older then and at least you'll have done as your Dad asked. Who knows by then they'll bring the voting age down to 18. There's been talk about it.

Then you'll be an adult and can do what you please.' He hugged me closer. My eyes filled with tears, tears of happiness this time.

I went home feeling elated, consoled and loving Tom even more. Though waiting to be able do what I wanted, and then only if they bring the age of voting down, it seemed an awful long time. I put my arms round myself hugging my body. Tom felt good without the rubbers. I began to feel a little anxious, I knew the risk of making love without protection. Surely just once you couldn't get pregnant, could you? I smiled as I thought about this and thought some more. I skipped the rest of the way home, happy in the knowledge that I might get pregnant and then Tom would have to marry me. Dad would make him, we would be able to get our own garage sooner than three years away and if Tom wanted well I could go to Wharton night school and learn the paperwork needed for the garage. Yes it would be perfect, it really would.

Ike was in the kitchen when I arrived home, he sat at the table staring down into a mug of tea.

'Alright Ike?' I asked breezily. I felt warm inside and memories of Tom surrounded me.

Ike looked up and stared at me. 'What you got to be so b...cheerful about?'

'Well the sun has been shining and all is good in the world and I am happy, that's what.' I smiled and put my arms round his thin shoulders to give him a hug.

'Ger off!' He said, shrugging my arms away.

'Ike?' I was bewildered, Ike often enjoyed a hug from his little sister, what had changed? What had changed the whole of him? He seemed so withdrawn and sullen. 'Missing Lily?'

'What!' His voice low and menacing. 'That bitch! I am glad to be shot of her!'

I cringed at the malice in his voice, I'd never heard Ike speak like that about anyone. Not even when I took his motorbike to bits. I drew back and stood by feeling so helpless. Ike stared at me and then suddenly smiled.

'Sorry our Ede. You look like I've just scared the hell out of you.'

I nodded, finding my voice, I asked gently, 'What's wrong Ike?'

'Life Ede, life. Not that I expect you to understand, you're young. Too young to understand relationships. Now then lass you get yourself to Wharton. Forget about lads. Sam hinted there might be one after you. Forget him, you hear! Time enough for that when you're older. Much older. You hear me?'

I nodded my heart in my mouth, any moment he would tell me he knew about Tom. But no, Sam had just hinted Ike said. 'Its OK Ike, I am going to Wharton. Just on my way to tell Dad.'

Ike nodded and I left him sitting in the kitchen, at the door I turned but he had his head in his hands. Perhaps he was ill. Why hadn't I asked him when we shared that moment just the two of us. I knew why, I was scared because of what he might tell me.

Dad looked up from the evening paper as I went into the living room. Mam and the kids could be heard upstairs and Sam was nowhere to be seen.

'Dad.' I spoke carefully choosing the right words to pacify him. 'I will go to Wharton, I think it would be good for me.'

Dad folded his paper and grinned, 'Good lass, there'll be no more talk about Farnley Hills then or the ridiculous idea of you wanting to become a mechanic.'

I shook my head. 'No Dad, I'll go to Wharton with Lucy and see if I like it.'

'You'll do the course Ede, no good starting and giving up because you don't like it. No one will want to give you a job if you quit a course.' Dad looked angry.

Why, oh why did I have to add the bit about if I'd like it? 'I will like it Dad. I will do the course.' I took a deep breath, might as well get it over with. 'Dad...I have a job for Saturdays and the holidays.'

'Good, good,' he looked pleased. 'Where then, in a shop I suppose? Which shop?'

Oh God this was harder than I thought. I closed my eyes for a moment, taking a deep breath, 'Not exactly a shop Dad, in a garage.'

'A what? Did you say garage, now look lass I've told you no more nonsense about mechanics!' He raised his voice and Mam came rushing through the door.

'Alf,' she said. 'I've just got the bairns settled will you keep your voice down!'

'Mam, I was just saying to Dad about my job.' I cried.

'Yes!' Yelled Dad, 'In a garage if you like.'

'Alf please keep it down and lets hear about this job Ede.' Mam looked at me quite alarmed, she knew of course I'd been helping out in the garage. But I don't think she had any idea it was going to be permanent. 'It's okay Mam,' I said more calmly than I felt. I had to get them agree to my little job. I was going to Wharton after all. 'Yes it's in a garage. But I have just told Dad I am going to Wharton. The job in the garage is helping with the paperwork. So will help me with my studies at Wharton. I'd like to focus on book keeping you see.' I kept my fingers crossed behind my back.

Mam looked so relieved she sat down with a sigh. 'That's so good Ede. Yes a job doing paperwork will help with your studies. Won't it Alf? It can only be good for her.'

'Mmm I suppose so.' Dad said in a resigned voice.

Mam looked at me, questions in her eyes, I knew she was going to ask what had made me change my mind about Wharton. I needed time to think about that. At that moment Shirley gave me the time as she screamed. 'I'll go Mam.' I said rushing to the door, I ran upstairs, to console what was just a toddler's bad dream. Settling Shirley back to sleep, I lay on my bed and thought about Tom. I wrapped my arms round my body imaging him to be close, touching me and loving me. 'Oh Tom Lister I do love you.' I breathed before falling asleep.

Hazel Stevens

5 - Ike's Recovery

Everything at home soon fell into a routine with Ike and the kids. Frankie was going to a nursery now and I was able to walk him there before I ran on to my school. Ike looked better and had started putting weight on. Mam said he was looking for a job. He soon found one at the mill. I'm sure Dad swayed it, though he vehemently denied having anything to do with it, Ike got the job on his own merits. Ike was to be a van driver for deliveries of woollen cloth made in the mill to various manufacturers around the West Riding of Yorkshire. He sometimes took shoddy out to the farms, this was the waste product, from the production of lower grade woollen cloth, that farmers used as manure. Ike told us he quite enjoyed driving out to the farms. Especially now spring was turning into summer. He would drive with his window down and one arm rested on it catching the sun. That arm would always be browner than the rest.

Sam always had a good suntan. I remained pale, I spent my time either in school or inside the garage helping Tom. He insisted I wore rubber gloves to keep my hands clean. As he said if I was supposed to be learning the book work, I wouldn't get oil on my hands.

I loved working alongside him. He taught me things about car engines and love making that I had never dreamed of. Despite my previous worries we often went to the barn on Saturday afternoons. He only worked Saturday mornings, but no need for the parents to know that I only worked that too.

Some afternoons we would drive up and away into the Yorkshire Dales, have a picnic by a babbling stream. I loved every minute. I even enjoyed my last weeks at school. Because we were leaving teachers were more relaxed and in many lessons we just played games.

Ike found a flat and moved into it. Mam told him firmly that he couldn't manage all the kids on his own so reluctantly he left the twins with us. Not ideal but at least I got my bedroom back. Sam moved into the front room and the twins had his.

Ike seemed happy and it wasn't long before he found a new girlfriend. Alice was pretty, small with a rounded figure and face. She had rosy cheeks and a bubbly nature. So very different to Lily. She doted on the kids and came with Ike every Friday to pick the twins up and take them back to Ike's to stay until Sunday. This arrangement made me feel less guilty about not being there to help Mam. I knew Saturdays would go back to as they were and sure enough she was soon catching the bus to Harrogate to see Great Aunt Eliza.

My Great Aunt was in her nineties and lived alone, managing all her own housekeeping and tending her small garden. Mam always came back with home grown fruit and veg, saying Aunt Eliza always grew far more than she could eat. She would regale how Aunt Eliza, despite her small garden grew such a lot in pots and troughs on the house wall. Mam would always finish off by saying she hoped she would be that fit when she got to her nineties. We all hoped so too.

One morning I had been longer than usual in the bathroom. I hadn't been feeling too well for a while now. Mam put it down to nerves at leaving school and going to Wharton. I guessed that was it, but I wasn't feeling nervous at all really. I couldn't wait for the summer holidays. Mam had agreed to have Frankie during the holidays. But as Conway was settled with his child minder, Ike said he could carry on there. He offered to send the twins, but no Mam wouldn't hear of it. She told him I would be home to help.

'My job Mam.' I complained, the previous evening.

'You won't be there everyday will you?' She'd replied. 'I mean its only a small place there can't be that much book keeping to do is there.' She looked at me accusingly.

'No, there won't.' Dad joined in. 'She'll be around plenty to help out, won't you Ede!'

It was a statement not a question, I bit my tongue and nodded, remembering what Tom had said about not rocking the boat. I suppose I could maybe persuade Mam to let me have a hour or two each day to go to the garage. I'd ask her when Dad wasn't around.

'Ede, what are you doing in there?' Mam rattled the bathroom door knob.

'Coming Mam.' I said pulling the door open, I leant on it as I felt so dizzy.

'Ede what on earth, my goodness girl you're as

white as a sheet. Get yourself to back to bed.'

I was so glad I felt better laid down, but felt so sick. Mam came in and asked what was wrong. I told her about the sickness. What had I'd been eating she asked me gently feeling my forehead. She shook her head as she could feel no fever. 'Stay in bed Ede. I'll bring you some tea and toast.'

The very thought had me jumping out of bed and hurrying to the bathroom. I felt better and to Mam's relief told her I would go to school.

It was the same next morning and on the third morning Mam said she would make me an appointment with the doctor.

I was so scared but the doctor told Mam he thought it was a sickness virus, it appeared there was a lot going round. I had to drink plenty and rest. So I had a wonderful three days off school.

Ike and Alice seemed really happy together and she gave him a purpose to life. The kids loved her too and we all welcomed her to the family. Alice became my friend. She wasn't much older than me and worked in the office at the mill. She had been to Wharton and had a lot of fun there. She told me I would too. It wasn't like school the tutors weren't as strict. I wanted to believe her but couldn't, I felt sure it would be an extension of school and just the same.

'Trust me Ede, it really is not a bit like school. You're there because you want to be there so it makes learning, well, seem better somehow, I guess its cos its what you want to do.' Alice assured me.

How could I tell her no, its definitely not what I want to do. She painted such a rosy picture, but I knew I would hate it. I so wanted to tell her but knew she'd tell Ike and then he would tell Dad.

'You okay Ede?' She asked me the following Sunday when they brought the twins back. 'Ike said you've had a sick bug?'

'Yes, much better now though.' I lied, as I was still having waves of feeling sick, quite a lot through the day now too. I knew I looked even paler than normal.

'A sick bug eh?' Alice said, she sounded suspicious and that worried me. It was just a sick bug, wasn't it.? What else could it be? I longed to ask. I had heard these bugs usually cleared up in one or two days but I'd felt ill all week. What was going on, what was wrong with me?

Alice asked if I would go to the shops with her. She said Ike had run out of soap powder and she wanted to get some and guessed Mr Patel's would still be open. We walked along to the little corner shop. Mr Patel was outside the shop washing the windows. I'm not sure now if he was officially open or not but he sold Alice the washing powder.

'I've something to tell you and ask you.' Alice said on our way home. She turned and looked curiously at me. 'Have you got a boyfriend?'

I nearly shook my head to deny it but I disparately needed someone to talk to. I wanted to tell the whole world about me and Tom. But I couldn't, Alice was different. Alice would understand I knew she loved Ike. I

Hazel Stevens

could see that by the way she looked at him. I nodded.

'Mmm I thought so,' she said taking hold of my arm. 'Ede, have you and this boy well done anything you shouldn't? You know what I mean don't you?'

I knew only too well and blushed, before saying 'No, I don't know what you mean.'

'Have you had sex?' Alice persisted.

I shook my head and turned away so she couldn't see my burning face.

'Ede tell me its important.' Alice pleaded. 'I won't say anything but its best you talk to someone. When was your last monthly?'

I turned back and stared at her. I couldn't actually say when that was. We'd had talks about it at school. The lads in the class always made a joke out of any sex education as it was then. I had my first monthly at fourteen. Been regular until... I knew I had to tell her, I needed to tell her.

'A...Alice.' I stuttered my face on fire. 'I don't know do you d...do you think I might be pregnant?' The words tumbled out and with it a great sense of relief. I had and hadn't really considered this possibility. I had hoped, but after seeing the doctor I dismissed the idea. Yet here was Alice asking me the most intimate of things. I just wanted to tell her, so I did tell her, all about Tom. My promise of a job in mechanics. Not wanting to go to Wharton. Everything how we planned to get a garage together. How much I loved him and he loved me. I grinned when I told her I hoped I was pregnant.

She grabbed me by the shoulders and shook me so

hard it brought tears to my eyes. 'Alice!'

'Oh Ede you stupid stupid girl! Hang on you say this boy works at a garage? Just how old is he Ede?'

I'd told her nearly everything so why hold back now. 'A bit older than Ike.'

Alice's face turned pale and she gasped. 'Ede he could go to jail for this.'

'No Alice.' I cried 'You've got it all wrong, he loves me, we're going to be married. What were you going to tell me Alice anyway?'

Alice hung her head for a moment and then told me her own happy news, Ike wanted to marry her. He was telling Mam and Dad at that very moment.

'Oh Alice how lovely.' I exclaimed giving her a hug. 'We could have a double wedding it would be perfect. Tom and Ike are pals you know. Alice I've always wanted a sister. Lily was horrible. But you're great Alice I'm so happy. Will you get pregnant soon then our babies can grow up together.' I knew I was gabbling but the news of Ike and Alice was so great and also thinking I might be pregnant, well that was great too. It was working out perfectly.

Alice shook her head and we walked home in silence, to be greeted by jubilant parents. They both threw their arms round Alice and said how wonderful Ike's news was.

'Just one problem though, Mam and Dad.' Ike's beaming smile fell. 'I have to divorce Lily, which as Alice knows isn't going to be easy I don't even know where Lily is.'

A debate followed on how they could find Lily and couldn't Ike just merely get a divorce on grounds of desertion. This seemed possible. Ike and Alice prepared to leave, even the kids seemed happy. Frankie announced Alice was his new Mum. Conway nodded and the twins just smiled not really knowing what was going on.

'Tell your Mam,' Alice mouthed to me as they left. I nodded half heartedly, I'd been turning over the things she had said about Tom and prison as we'd walked home. I was worried. I needed to find out if I was definitely pregnant. I would also tell Tom before anyone else anyway. I smiled at my big brother as he bent to kiss me on the cheek. He had recovered well and we all knew Alice would make him happy. That was the best thing in the world right at that moment.

6 - Telling Tom

As the days turned into a week and Alice was due again that Sunday to bring the twins back, I tried my hardest to be excused from the ritual, as it had become, family tea. Mam wouldn't hear of it.

I prayed Alice hadn't told Ike. My prayers were answered. She looked at me inquisitively over the table for a few moments. 'How are you Ede? Over the sick bug?'

I nodded, yes I felt much better the sickness was still there a little in the morning but not as bad as it was.

'You still look a bit peaky, doesn't she Ike?' Alice smiled.

Ike nodded and then went on debating with Dad about rugby versus football. Ike had always been a Leeds United football fan. But Dad was more into rugby and they usually had these big debates. Well they used to when Ike lived at home, it was lovely to see our Ike back to normal and the debates and banter reinstated.

On their way out to go home, Alice secretly pressed a card into my hand. I quickly stuffed it into my shirt before anyone noticed. Later I retrieved it and saw the address and number of a Family Planning clinic. Alice had scribbled on the bottom that she would come with me if I wanted.

I sighed with relief she obviously hadn't told Ike, or

he would have said something and the darling girl was offering to help. Tears sprang to my eyes, I was so glad Ike had found someone as lovely as Alice. She was our sort, down to earth and always looked happy. I think it was because of her frothy blonde hair and rosy cheeks.

I met her from work the next day and we arranged the two of us would go to the clinic the next Saturday morning. I longed to tell Tom but I wanted to be absolutely sure first.

I told Tom I had to stay at home to look after the twins that Saturday morning. Mam had to go to see Great Aunt Eliza, who wasn't very well. The latter was true, but of course he asked why Ike wasn't having the twins, I quickly thought up the excuse that he was working overtime.

I told Mam and Dad, Alice was taking me shopping, for some new clothes for college. Dad thrust five pounds in my hand telling me to treat myself.

I pushed it back to him, 'We're only going to have a look Dad.'

He laughed and insisted I take it and buy something with it.

I nodded guiltily, no use buying new clothes because they won't fit me for a while. Shoes I decided would be a safe bet, I would buy shoes and I knew I would have enough left to treat Alice. She was turning out to be a great friend and as I felt then very much an ally.

The building was grey and austere, inside the walls were light green. An official looking lady sat upright behind a table we assumed was the reception desk. 'Yes,' she barked in a harsh voice.

I cowered behind Alice, who, bless her, was requesting a pregnancy test for me. My eyes darted round the waiting room in case there was someone I knew. I breathed a sigh of relief as the three girls sitting in the waiting area were strangers.

It wasn't long before my name was called. Alice and I went into an examination room.

A woman in a white coat asked if I had brought a sample. I shook my head not quite realising what she meant. Alice explained and the woman held out a bottle to me and asked me to get do one. She pointed to a door in the corner of the room.

I returned the bottle to her and she dipped paper in it. 'Well, yes looks like it could be. I'd better examine you.'

I lay on the couch holding my breath while she prodded and poked. She squeezed my stomach and asked questions. I blandly answered.

'Well,' she said after prodding me again. 'Yes there is a foetus in there, you'll be about eight weeks maybe ten.' She peered at Alice a question hanging on her lips. 'I know someone who can help with this accident.' Turning back to me she asked 'How old are you exactly?'

'Sixteen.' Alice replied for me a little too quickly.

'The name of your doctor?'

'She hasn't got one yet, a doctor I mean.' Alice said guardedly. 'She has just moved in with her brother and me, haven't got round to registering her yet.'

I was amazed at the story Alice told this woman, who looked rather suspicious to say the least. Alice asked her for the name of the person who could help and told her we'd be in touch when I was registered with a doctor. The woman nodded and told me to get dressed.

'Alice, you were wonderful.' I hugged her once we were outside.

'Cup of tea needed, look there's a café across the road. We need to talk,' she pulled me across through the café door and we sat down at an empty table, ordering tea from the hovering waitress.

I listened to her over the cup of tea, which remained untouched. I couldn't believe my ears hearing what Alice was saying. The name she had been given, which I thought was a mother and baby clinic, was someone who could get rid of my baby for me. My throat dried and I stared at Alice as she was offering to pay. 'No one would ever need know,' she added.

'I'd know...' I stammered out at last. 'No! Alice No! I won't get rid of Tom's baby.'

Alice resumed her lecture this time telling me I would be ruining my life, Tom wouldn't want me. He'd been using me. No one would want a girl with a baby. I had college to think of. My parents, the shame it would bring. She went on and on. I couldn't stand it any more. I pushed my chair back and hurried out into the street. Tears blurred my vision but I ran as far away from her as fast as I could, I thought she was my ally. Some joke that was!

I needed Mam, so I ran home and flung myself into her arms. Sobbing. She held me close for quite a few minutes, waiting for my sobs to decrease.

'Ede what on earth?' She asked quietly.

Tell her, I told myself, tell her. So I did between great gulping sobs. She sat me down at the kitchen table and put the kettle on. She didn't say a word until she had two cups of tea on the table and she sat down herself. 'Ede. Oh my dear girl, were you forced, do you know what I mean?'

I shook my head. She asked if I knew for certain, had I been to see our doctor. I told her about Alice, the clinic and Alice wanting me to have an abortion. 'I can't Mam I really can't!'

'You can't what?' Dad coming in through the back door, made Mam and I jump. We'd not heard the back gate or his footsteps. Neither of us answered him.

'Can't what?' He repeated. 'If this is about not going to Wharton...'

Mam broke him off shaking her head, telling him to sit down. Sam came in asking if there was tea going as he saw our cups on the table.

Mam rose and got two more cups out for them. 'Going to have to tell them Ede.'

Sam and Dad turned to me expectantly. 'Tell us what?' They both said in unison.

Sitting across the table from them, my whole body was shaking, I hung my head so they couldn't see the tears.

'Has someone died?' Asked Sam in a half joky manner.

'What is it lass?' Dad spoke so softly and kindly.

I couldn't bear it. I sobbed, laying my head on the table, my body heaving.

'She's pregnant.' I raised my head, it wasn't Mam who'd said the words but Ike. He stood in the back doorway. The anger in his face had turned it red. He strode towards me. I jumped up and backed away. Mam grabbed him, he roughly pushed her aside. Sam rose quickly and thrust an arm round Ike's neck. 'This'll solve nowt Ike,' he hissed.

Dad stood up too and backed away from the table, from me.

'Who is he? Who is the bastard? I'll kill him, after I kill her.' Ike screamed, Sam was on his tip toes reaching up, his arm tight round Ike's shoulders.

Dad sat back down, he put his head in his hands. 'I don't believe this Ede, you're too young. Lib fetch the police. Who is he Ede, the police will want to know? You have to tell us girl,' he sounded angry, very angry. Although his tone was low and steely I looked up and saw a deep sadness in his face.

What had I done to my family? To make Ike so mad he wanted to kill me and Dad so sad. I began to cry again and Mam came to me and asked me gently to tell them the name of the lad responsible. I shook my head. 'Please, no police.' I sobbed. 'He loves me and will marry me, I know that. He will Mam honest he will, it will be fine and what we both wanted.'

Ike screamed again. 'You stupid daft bitch. How old are you? This lad'll be same age, how can he afford to get married? How can he support you? Same ger off me will you!'

Sam held on as Ike made another attempt to get round the table to me. He shook his head. I knew Sam had guessed who the Father might be, I didn't want to be there when he told my parents and Ike.

I looked beseechingly at Mam, she too had thrown herself at Ike as again he tried to break free and get to me.

'Go upstairs Ede,' she said. I didn't need telling twice. I left the scene of chaos in our kitchen.

Dad, his head in his hands, Mam and Sam holding onto Ike for dear life, who was still muttering death threats. I ran upstairs to the bolt hole, the bathroom, and rammed the lock home. I'd be safe here for a while and when all had quietened down I could sneak out and tell Tom before he left work. My sobbing abated and I sat on the lino floor, by the door, listening. I heard Sam come upstairs and go into his room. Thank goodness that the kids weren't here. I guess Alice was minding all four of them. Ike wouldn't stay long. Hearing the back door slam, I cautiously opened the bathroom door and crept downstairs. Mam and Ike were in the living room. Dad was nowhere to be seen. I pressed my body against the hall wall and listened. Mam was talking softly, begging Ike to calm down.

'I can't calm down Mam.' Ike said. 'How could our

Ede be so stupid? She's just a child, no one will want to marry her and then where will she be? Alice said she had told Ede to have an abortion. That's the best thing Mam. Honest it is. Please don't look at me like that. It's not murder why, the thing is just a thing.'

'How can you say that? It's a child, anyway I know our Ede won't hear of it.' Mam told him.

I nodded, wishing I had the courage to go in there and face Ike tell him myself.

What he said next really shook me and I think it did Mam too.

'You don't understand Mam, Lily did that. Told me she was on the pill. I didn't know any different, thought it was easy for women to get that now. But she got pregnant, just so I would marry her and she could get away from her Dad. Right mean old bastard he is. Used to beat the living daylights out of all of them. She was scared to death of him. I knew Lily didn't really love me or want me. She just wanted a way out and I obliged.'

I could sense Mam holding him as he revealed what a travesty his marriage to Lily was.

I took my chance and quietly crept past the living room open door and out through the back door, into the alley and ran to Tom. He would stand up to Ike, tell him we loved each other and he would stand by me. Marry me, tell them all of our plans. Sam might open up and tell them he'd been seeing Phyllis. He didn't think I knew. But I'd seen them standing close together at the bus stop once. They hadn't seen me and I said nothing. Sam had told us that Saturday afternoon he was working over. I kept the revelation to myself. I could use it if he threatened to reveal who the father of my baby was.

Tom looked up as I dashed in. I threw myself into his arms, ignoring the grease on his hands and overalls.

'Eeh up lass what's to do now then?' He pushed me away, frowning when he saw my tear stained face. 'Come on Ede, why you been crying?'

It was now or never, but I wasn't afraid, I knew he'd be happy. All the same I still stammered out the words. 'I...I...Tom I'm pregnant.' I said at last. There now he knew.

The questions came next which took me completely by surprise. How did I know? Was I sure? How far? Definitely his? I backed away at the last question. How could he think that? Seeing my horrified face he apologised immediately. He didn't look happy or excited like I thought he would. He looked more shocked than anything. I tried to speak to tell him it was okay, we'd be okay. The words wouldn't come. He didn't come and swing me round in joy as I imagined. He just stood staring at me with shock and horror in his face. I could see that all too clearly. Alice had been right all along he didn't really want me. He didn't want to marry me. He'd said those things to get what he wanted. He wasn't going to stand up to Dad, Ike or anyone.

I turned and ran out of the garage. I didn't hear him calling my name. I just wanted to be as far away from him, my family, everyone. I ran out of the street, down the main road and away. Yes I would go away, stuff them all, I'd be okay on my own. I didn't need anyone. I'd stopped running now. The houses turned into countryside as I walked swiftly on. I needed a bolt hole for now, until I made a plan on what to do next. I knew just where to find one too. I realised I was going in the right direction. Picking up my pace I started running again, running as if my life depended on it and in a way it did or at least my baby's life.

7 - He Doesn't Want Me

I found myself on the Kirkstall road, not sure if I had gone there accidently or what. I needed a drink, the barn, water in the stream by the barn was clear enough and I was sure it would be okay.

To my annoyance I heard giggling coming from inside the barn. I walked up stream a little way. Obviously it wasn't just mine and Tom's secret place. I sat down by a big oak tree, glad the grass was dry. I could see the barn round the side of the tree trunk, but I knew I would be hidden from whoever was in there. I sat for what seemed like hours waiting for them to leave. My mind full of thoughts about what to do next.

It was clear Tom didn't want me. So I had to form some kind of a plan. Should I go to Alice and ask for her help to get rid of my baby. I felt sick just thinking about it. This was a life inside me. I couldn't do that, would never do it. I was shocked that someone in authority would even suggest it to Alice too. I thought they were there to help girls like me. Jenny Grimshaw had become pregnant at fourteen and she kept the baby. Her Mother told everyone it was hers, but we all knew it was really Jenny's. Abortion was illegal and I'd heard, from girls at school, that witches in the back streets did them.

A young couple came out of the barn hand in hand, the girl smoothing her hair down with the other hand, the lad looked pleased with himself. She stopped and turned to kiss him, but he carried on walking and their hands fell apart. The girl ran to catch him up and I could see her talking animatedly to him. He shrugged his shoulders and walked on. I felt so sorry for her as she continued after him, where was her pride. Her childhood taken. I hoped she wouldn't end up pregnant and alone like me.

I made my way into the barn, hugging myself as I lay in the hay. 'Tom, Tom.' I moaned, remembering the afternoons we spent there together. I let the tears roll for a while before sitting up telling myself to forget him.

My thoughts moved on, who I could turn to for help. Lucy? She had always been my best friend, well until lately. She had scorned at the way I didn't want to go to Wharton. Laughed when I told her of my love for Tom. She would be horrified at me having a baby. Horrified yes, but would she help me now? No. I decided definitely not.

Sadie? We had become quite close, but I thought she would be very judgemental. No matter how broad minded her views were. Surely though she would understand. Wouldn't she? She could talk to Tom, make him see how much I loved him. How...

I could see the futility in my thoughts, as my Dad would say, 'you have made your bed and you must lie on it.' The tears came again as I thought about my Dad and Mam. I realised I had been so stupid. But I still couldn't and wouldn't do as they wanted me to. Could I? Could I get rid of my unborn child? Ike said it was just a thing, I knew from pictures shown to us in school that it was only tiny, had no real features or limbs. I also knew that I would regret for the rest of my life denying this child life. I would constantly be thinking, as each year came round, what the child would be like. No I could not and would not do as they wanted.

I knew though I would need some help. I couldn't do this on my own, could I? I would stay in the barn for the night and hope someone came to mind who would help me. Before darkness fell I went outside and had another drink from the stream. I also gathered some green black berries, gulping them down to try and ease my hunger. For once the nausea I had been having wasn't affecting me that afternoon and I was glad about that.

I lay back and grabbed some of the loose hay to cover myself. Staring at the darkening roof beams. Noises began. Rustling in the far corner and tiny squeaks. I peered into the gloom and saw what I thought were mice scurrying about. Suddenly something flew out above my head and I ducked. It disappeared through a small opening in the barn wall. Another followed, then another. Birds? What birds flew out at dusk? Owls? No, these were too small for owls. I shuddered when I realised they were bats.

I could hear strange noises coming from outside and it took a while till I recognised the soft mooing of cows in the distance and the bleat of a stray lamb closer to the barn. A grunting came closer to the barn door. What was that? I held my breath until I heard it shuffle away.

Would the noises ever stop? I sat up arms clasping my knees, peering round warily, as night closed in. Louder rustling came nearer to me now. I screamed as something ran over my feet. It was too large to be a mouse, what then? I listened again, holding my breath. All became silent for a while. My scream must have scared the creatures in the barn as much as they scared me. It wasn't long before the rustling resumed, again I screamed, once more all became still. I sat rocking backwards and forwards. I couldn't go on like this all night, could I? One thing was certain I felt so scared of the things around me and what my future held. I knew I would not sleep at all that night.

Part Three

1 - Gone Missing

It was tea time and Ede hadn't returned home. Mam and Dad were in the kitchen obviously discussing Ede's situation. Ike had gone back to his flat where Alice and the children would be waiting. How Mam managed to calm him down I don't know. I've never seen him so angry not even after the motorbike incident. He wasn't even angry at Lily when he came home. Subdued, yes, which went on for weeks. Since Alice came into his life, he was back to the Ike we all knew and loved. I looked up to him in more ways than one. He had my admiration for the way he was dealing with being a single parent, despite all the help Mam gave him. Ike had made a real home for himself and the kids.

I was dumbfounded though at Our Ede's stupidity, getting herself pregnant at her age it was completely irresponsible of them both. By, I was going to give Tom Lister a piece of my mind when I saw him.

I cautiously went into the kitchen Mam and Dad looked up at me. Mam had been crying, her eyes were red and her cheeks tear stained. Dad stared at me, his face white, his lips pressed together, the lines on his face seemed highlighted somehow.

'Do you know where she'll have gone Sam?' Mam asked her voice shaking.

I shook my head, oh I knew already, but I wasn't going to let on. As I knew they would go mad if they knew I even had an inkling of what my sister was up to. I would get the blame for not telling them or even stopping Ede from seeing Lister. How could I tell them that I had tried? They know how strong minded she was and in my eyes foolish too. I would go, find her and bring her home. Hopefully make her see sense, no matter how awful it was, she just had to get rid of the baby.

'I'll go round to Lucy's, see if she's there shall I?'

Mam and Dad nodded in unison, I pulled my jacket off the hook on the back door. I'd no idea how long I would be, getting my jacket though was an automatic reaction. I was glad I had got it as I stepped outside, it started spotting with gentle rain. I passed Lucy's gate and carried on down our road. I knew Ede wouldn't be there.

Ten minutes later and I picked my way to the front door of the Lister household. They had a small front garden littered with rubbish. The flaking paint on the door drifted towards me as I knocked on it, more loudly than I intended. I took a step back and surveyed the rest of the house. The net curtains looked at least clean, despite the peeling paint round the windows.

I had seen Phyllis a few times, not intentionally, courage failed me to ask her out on a date. We'd met at the shops and in the street. I'd never been to her house, though everyone knew where the Listers lived so I needed no directions.

I knocked again, surely someone must be in on a Saturday afternoon. Phyllis would be at work though. She told me she had finally found a job in a chemist's shop in the city centre. I was pleased for her. I guessed it would be hard to find something with the family's name and reputation hanging over her.

The door groaned open and Mrs Lister stood there. 'Who've we got 'ere then?' She asked grinning at me.

'Do you know Ede Wagstaff? I...I...well is our Ede, is she here?' I gabbled.

'Ah yes.' Mrs Lister smiled. 'I know Ede, what do you want with her lad?'

'She...she's my sister. I want to know if she is here?'

Mrs Lister shook her head, 'No, not here but if she comes I'll tell her you're looking for her, shall I?'

'Yes, please.' I nodded and turned, then quickly spun back. 'Is Tom in?'

She nodded and shouted over her shoulder for her eldest son.

He came ambling down the hall, with a mug of tea in his hand. 'Now then young Sam and what can I do for you?'

'I think you've done enough, don't you?' I snarled.

Mrs Lister looked alarmed at my tone of voice and opened her mouth to speak. Tom cut her off. 'It's Okay Ma, I'll deal with this.' He pushed me into the road and followed, slamming the door behind him, almost in his Mother's bewildered face.

I was scared at his reaction. I thought he would hit me. But instead he said in a soft voice. 'What you doing here?'

'I...I...came...looking for our Ede.' I managed to speak at last.

'Ede?' His voice was low, 'Why would she be here?'

I realised seeing the concerned look on his face, he wasn't going to belt me. So I told him what I knew. How Ede had been in a right state, Ike being furious and Ede running off.

'We know she's pregnant Lister. How could you? She's fifteen for God's sake.' I raised my voice in anger at him. So what if he did hit me. At that moment I didn't care. I was so mad he had taken advantage of my little sister.

'Now hang on Sam. We were careful,' he said, as if that made it all right. 'Where is she? What happened?'

I shook my head saying she'd gone off without us realising and that I assumed she had gone to see him.

He nodded and admitted she had and he felt that he had handled her news all wrong. 'I was so shocked Sam. It was the last thing I wanted to hear just then,' he held his hands up in surrender. 'Hold on Sam before you start having another go. I love Ede I really do. She means the world to me. I never intended it to happen, fall in love I mean. But I did and I think she loves me. Or rather did love me, I think her news may have made her think I don't want her. I'll find her Sam. I promise and when I do I'll bring her home.'

'They don't know.'

'They don't know what Sam?'

'That you're the Father.'

'Oh.' Tom ran his hands through his hair. 'Well, I guess it's gotta come out sooner or later, hasn't it?'

I shrugged my shoulders. 'You could get into trouble with the police.' I added lamely.

Tom nodded, 'Look, lets worry about that when it happens, right now we'd better find Ede before something happens to her or she does something stupid.'

I agreed and we parted company, I would go and ask Lucy. She would know of Ede's other friends who she might have gone to.

I half wondered if Tom would go and look for her, was he just saying he loved her to pacify me, make an excuse for getting her pregnant. He'd gone back into the house and shut the door. I started walking down the street, I'd only gone a couple of paces when I heard the door open and close again. Tom came out and quickly walked the other way. He was certainly going somewhere in a hurry, was it to look for Ede though?

Lucy had no idea where Ede might be but she gave me a couple of names and addresses of girls she thought Ede was pals with, one of them was Sadie Lister.

I knew all about Sadie and Ede being friends. Lucy told me Ede was with Sadie now more than her. I could see the sadness in Lucy's face. Ede and Lucy had grown up together, how could my sister abandon her for a Lister?

I called in home to see if Ede had returned. Mam was there on her own.

'You're Dad's gone round to talk to Ike, he thinks she might have gone there. I doubt it though Sam. The way Ike reacted he would be the last person she would go to. I'm not sure about Alice though.'

I nodded in agreement after Ike's reaction it certainly would be the last place on earth Ede would want to be. Mam and I knew she had developed a close friendship with Alice and I could see Mam's reasoning that she might have gone to Alice. But not at Ike's anyway.

'Ike will want to look for her,' Mam continued. 'I'm sure of that, it's because of his reaction why she has gone. Poor lass. We'll sort it out. I'd best stay here in case she comes back. Will...will you go and find her Sam?'

I nodded and showed her the list of names Lucy provided and told Mam I'd start with them.

After an hour of knocking on doors, asking the same question, I returned home feeling helpless and annoyed. Dad was back with Ike, they had looked round the shops. We sat round the table drinking cups of tea Mam had made. Ike was sure she'd be home when she was hungry. Mam wanted to phone the police. Ike calmed her down saying they wouldn't do anything till she'd been gone twenty four hours.

'Ike!' Mam sobbed. 'My baby can't stay out all night. We've got to find her.'

'Some baby...' Ike muttered, he broke off as I kicked him under the table. His scowl told me he was not best pleased I'd done that but he said no more.

'What are we to do then?' I asked.

The three of them stared at me, before Ike said. 'Wait.'

2 - Restless Night

Dad had gone round the list of friends I gave him again. Still no joy and he commented how no one had seen her. Also he would know, he said, if they had been lying to cover her.

Mam spent most of the evening crying. She went into the kitchen to make a pot of tea. Dad and I looked at each other when we heard the back door close. We jumped up and headed out into the yard.

'Libby.' Dad shouted. 'Come back, it's dark, you won't know where to go.' He ran after Mam as she hurried down the back alley.

I stood feeling helpless as I saw him catch up with her and put his arms round her. I could hear the sobs heaving themselves out of her body as Dad drew her back up the alley. 'Mam.' was all I could say as resignedly, she allowed Dad to lead her back to the house. I reached my arm out and touched her shoulder. She looked at me with blank eyes. At that moment I realised Mam was getting older, the lines on her once clear face now finely etched. I noticed too in the dim light from our open back door the grey in her hair. I don't think I had seen that before.

I cursed our Ede inwardly, she had done this. She had brought this tormented look in Mam's eyes. I followed them into the kitchen, muttering that I felt sure Ede was okay. Dad nodded. In my head I thought she would be, she must surely have met up with her lover and no doubt they were planning their rosy little future together. I'd give her rosy when I caught up with her!

Dad led Mam upstairs and I followed, hoping Mam would get some sleep.

I woke in the early hours of the morning, hearing Dad call 'Lib, Lib where are you?'

I shot up out of bed and hurried onto the landing, Dad was coming back upstairs shaking his head. I followed him into the bedroom. 'Mam?'

'She's not here son. Get dressed, we have to find her, before she goes missing too. Oh my God what a mess,' he waved me away.

I dressed in seconds and followed Dad downstairs and out into the cool night air. 'Where shall we go Dad?' My voice quavered with worry.

'You go round Bean Street way, up past you Granddad's place and I'll go round the other way and meet you at the park gates.

I reached the gates long before Dad and peered into the darkness. I wanted to go and look but I knew I had to wait for Dad. After all, he might have found her.

Someone came hurrying down the road. 'Dad is that you?' I called anxiously, 'Have you found her?'

'No son, do you think she'll be in there?' He nodded his head towards the park.

I nodded, Mam might think Ede would hide there. 'Shall we split up?'

'Shh.' Dad whispered, 'What's that?'

I strained my ears and the soft muffled sound of

crying came to us over the early morning air. 'Mam.' I called, 'Mam, oh Mam, is that you, where are you?'

The crying became sobs, we followed the sound and I heard Mam call, 'Sam.' We found her hunched on a bench by the lake. 'I looked all over the park, thought she might be here.' Mam sobbed out.

Dad put his arm round her and said he was taking her home. I paused unsure what to do, should I carry on searching the park. 'You too Sam. Home now. We all need rest and we can come and look again tomorrow,' he sounded so calm and orderly. His only daughter was out in the night somewhere, how could he be like that I wondered?

'Alf our baby...' Mam broke into sobs again, pulling away from him, desperate to get back to her search, however fruitless it might be.

'Lib, home.' Dad said and reluctantly Mam let him lead her away through the streets to number one Congleton Terrace.

I woke wearily, Mam and Dad were already up. Still no sign of Our Ede. I asked if Ike would be bringing the twins back later. Dad told me no, they were staying at Ike's. Ike was going out to look for Ede, Alice was looking after the kids. I marvelled at the way this girl had taken Ike and Lily's kids to her heart. They adored her and she them. It was lovely to see how quickly she had become Mum to all four of them. Only Frankie was a little hesitant with her. He was old enough to remember his own Mother of course. However day by day we witnessed him growing closer to Alice.

Hearing the back gate open I leapt to the door, if this was my sister I wanted to get in first to give her a piece of my mind. Lucy jumped back in alarm as I flung open the door.

'Is she back home yet Sam?' She asked quietly.

I shook my head, did she know something she hadn't let on last night? I asked her. Lucy looked sad and worried.

'No,' she said slowly, 'but there has been something bothering her for a while. I couldn't get it out of her Sam, I tried honest I did. I think she has been seeing a boy, well a man, for the past few months. When we girls, you know, talk about boys we like. Ede wouldn't join in, when I asked her why, she shrugged and said she couldn't be bothered with boys. Too childish she said. I just thought I should tell you Sam.'

I could see Lucy felt uncomfortable and I had the feeling she knew only too well who Ede was seeing, but she didn't want to say.

'Perhaps them at the garage might know,' Lucy added sheepishly.

It took me all my strength not to blurt it out that I knew all about her and her 'boy' friend! Instead I told her thanks and I hadn't thought of the garage, I would go there straight away.

Mam looked even worse and much, much older that morning. She obviously hadn't slept. I left them phoning the police. It wasn't twenty four hours but I knew they both felt they had to do something, get advice and help looking for her. I gave a wry smile as I thought what would the neighbours say when a police car rolled up to ours.

I didn't expect to find Tom Lister at work, it was Sunday but you never knew. The garage was closed up and the door padlocked. I made my way to the Lister house. The curtains were closed and it was obvious everyone was in bed. I knocked loudly on the door, jumping back as flakes of paint headed my way again.

In just a few seconds it opened and Phyllis peered round the edge of it. She clutched a pink dressing gown round her when she saw it was me and opened the door further. 'Sam, oh Sam. What are you doing here?' She asked. 'Has Ede turned up yet? No sorry daft question she can't have done or you wouldn't be here.'

She sounded so kind and caring, I shook my head as words wouldn't come. I just wanted to take her in my arms, just as I thought that the most unexpected thing happened, Phyllis stepped out of the door and put both her arms round me. 'Dear Sam, you look so worried,' she whispered, I felt her lips kiss my hair. I raised my arms and held her tight, it felt so good. Something I wanted to do for a long time and now I wanted to kiss her. I stopped myself knowing it was not the time or the place.

'Is Tom here?' I murmured into her lovely fresh smelling blonde hair. I didn't want to break away from the embrace but knew I must. I held her from me at arms length, I repeated the question.

'He was,' she said soothingly.

I baulked 'Trust him to have a good nights sleep!'

'Sam, Sam,' she cried. 'He didn't! He's been out all night I promise you that, our Sadie too, both of them looking for Ede. I'm sorry I didn't go but I had no idea where to look. Tom came home got changed and has gone back out again. Sadie's in bed, she's exhausted.'

I stared at her in disbelief. Her family had been out all night looking for Ede. 'Where's he gone Phyllis?' I released my grip on her arms as I saw her wince. I'd obviously held onto this fragile girl too tightly. 'I'm sorry Phyllis.' I added as I saw her rubbing her arms.

'I'm not sure Sam, he did say something about the country.'

'The country, what country? Does he think she's gone abroad? Surely not, how could she?' The questions flooded my head. Maybe they had planned this, they would elope abroad.

'No, countryside Sam, not abroad.' Phyllis interrupted my whirling mind.

'Where, do you know where?' I asked fervently now. If I could reach Ede before him I could and would stop their little plan of eloping. Thinking rationally perhaps it would be the best step for them both. Could you get married at fifteen without parents permission? I doubted it but Ede would be sixteen soon, they would lie low till her birthday. I was sure that was their plan.

Phyllis shook her head 'It could be anywhere Sam, couldn't it? I don't know, I really don't,' she smiled sympathetically.

Oh how I wanted to kiss those lips. 'Thanks Phyllis.' I muttered turning away. I reluctantly took my leave and left her standing on the doorstep. I knew she was still there as I walked down the road. I hadn't heard the door close. I so wanted to turn and wave, blow her a kiss, let her know how I felt. But I couldn't, I just couldn't. I would have to forget Phyllis Lister. One member of the Lister family had caused enough trouble for us as it was. Yes I would put her out of my mind. I couldn't though, I remembered and felt her embrace all that day.

Ike was at home when I got back, he'd been out early looking too. He looked tired and I heard him saying it was all his fault. If he hadn't been so angry about her being pregnant she wouldn't have run off. 'Have you any news Sam?' He asked wearily.

I shook my head and told them about Lucy and the suggestion about the garage. How I'd gone there but it was locked so I went to the Lister's, I concluded holding my breath.

'Why would you go to that house?' Dad roared, his face red with anger.

'Well Dad.' I began hesitantly, knowing I couldn't tell him the whole truth. I just daren't. 'Tom Lister works at the garage our Ede has been going to on Saturdays.'

'My girl, my girl,' he stood up now. 'Has been working in the same place as a Lister! I won't have that! I really won't!'

Mam pushed him back into the chair telling him to calm down, the police had arrived. Dad did as she bade him and she nodded to me to let the police in.

After Dad told her about Ede's disappearance. The softly spoken Irish police woman shook her head. 'It's early yet,' she said sympathetically. 'I'll put in a report of course, but we can't do anything till this afternoon. Are you sure there was nothing bothering her?'

I wanted to tell them everything and half opened my mouth to speak. Dad's eyes made me close it again. 'Well,' he said. 'No more than the usual teenage tiff about make up and things.'

Make up! I wanted to scream, surely he should tell them the truth. They would know who in the area performed abortions. Ede could have gone to one of them. They could look for her there. I kept quiet, as they said there was nothing they could do till later.

'Look I'm sorry, I really am,' the police woman said. 'Its obviously just a tiff and I am sure she'll be home by dinner time. She'll be at a friends as we speak.'

Dad told her we had asked all her friends twice. He gave her the list and she thanked him saying they could use that later if she hadn't appeared. She felt positive Ede would be back by dinner. She left telling us all to get some sleep, as we looked exhausted, had we been up all night? We nodded and agreed sleep was needed.

After she left Dad took Mam back upstairs. Ike and I looked at each other.

'Get yerself some sleep too Sam,' he said, standing up and opening the back door.

'You going home Ike?' I quizzed.

He nodded, 'Got my own family to think of, give

us a bell when she turns up. First though, I might pay Lister a call.'

'It's no good Ike,' I said quietly. 'I've just been there, he's not there.' My voice shook, I just daren't tell him the truth. My brother was getting his life back on track, if he knew about Tom Lister I couldn't be sure what he would do.

'Oh well,' Ike sighed. 'Get some rest, I'll get home.'

I nodded dumbly, everyone seemed so calm. I couldn't go to bed, someone had to be here when she did finally turn up. Perhaps fatigue and worry had overcome them all. I couldn't understand how they could simply just go off to bed and home. I knew in the back of my mind Ede would be with Tom and would at least be okay. I hoped so anyway. But he'd been out all night Phyllis said and hadn't found her. I should go out and look again, but where? Perhaps Tom would find her at this barn. Phyllis hadn't a clue where it was, pity she hadn't thought to ask him. No don't blame Phyllis, I scolded myself. I went into the living room and lay on the couch. My mind not on Ede but Phyllis. It wasn't long before tiredness got the better of me and I closed my eyes.

Hazel Stevens

3 - Still No Sign

A door banged and I woke up with a start. 'Ede.' I called out. There was no reply and I jumped as Dad appeared from upstairs.

'Is she back?' He asked smoothing down his ruffled hair. Sleep still in his eyes, he peered at the clock on the mantle piece. It was only ten thirty. If Dad felt like me, it seemed we'd been asleep for hours.

'No.' I replied lifting, what felt like, my very heavy body off the couch. 'Tea Dad? Shall I make Mam a cup too?'

'Thanks son a cup of tea would be grand. Mam's still asleep so leave hers in the pot. I'm sure she'll be up soon.'

I went into the kitchen and smiled as I filled the electric kettle, remembering Ede's treatment of Mam's first kettle. It had to be got rid of after Ede's meddling, as it continued to leak.

Dad had tried to fix it but hadn't been able to. He threatened to dock Ede's pocket money, but I don't think he ever did.

Placing a mug of tea in his hand I sat down beside him. Neither of us spoke, just sipped the hot tea as if it would make it all better.

'Where can she be Sam?' Dad sighed, his voice thick. Anger had left him in his sleep and he looked so sad.

'I don't know Dad.' I said honestly.

'I...think I might know someone who might...'

'I thought you'd asked everyone!'

'Well yes I did, but I'm sorry Dad. I...think Tom Lister might know.'

'Lister! What's he got to do with it?' Dad stood up and put his mug on the mantlepiece.

'Lister!' He repeated.

I nodded and explained that I thought Ede might have a crush on him.

Dad sat down beside me. 'You don't think it was this Lister that raped our Ede do you? I'll bloody well hang for the bugger.'

I was shocked Dad never swore like that. 'No I'm sure he wouldn't.'

'How can you be sure Sam? I'm going round there now!' He stood up and strode out of the house slamming the door behind him.

That must have woke Mam up as I heard her call 'Alf, is that Ede home?'

I ran upstairs, told her what I had told Dad and he was on his way to the Listers. I added he wouldn't find Tom there. How I'd been and Tom was out looking for Ede.

'Mam, Dad thinks Tom might have raped Ede.'

'Oh surely not. Well he's...' Her voice trailed off as she thought about the consequences. I knew I had to tell her.

'No Mam, I am sure he didn't rape her.' I told her how I knew that Ede and Tom had been carrying on for a while now.

'No, Sam...he's well...he's a man. He must have forced her.'

I shook my head and told her about the condom. 'I think Ede has done it with her eyes open and willingly too.'

Mam's face paled and she looked down. Her hands twisted the bed sheet. 'She's fifteen,' was all she said, before shooing me out the bedroom telling me she wanted to get dressed.

I made my way downstairs, hoping Phyllis hadn't answered the door and been at the end of my Dad's rage. I wanted to go after him, protect Phyllis. I wanted to stay with Mam though, she looked so ill. I sat at the kitchen table waiting.

It was gone eleven thirty before Dad came back. Mam was busying herself in the kitchen making dinner. Dad slammed the back door behind him as he came in.

'The little hussy!' He yelled. 'Seems from what Lister says Ede has been there several times with that bloody son of his! Welcome too he said! In love they are, he said! She's a child Lib, doesn't know what love is! I could have laid him out the smug look on his face. If it hadn't been for Margaret I would have done too! I bet it was his lad that forced her! By he'll pay for this! With a prison sentence if I have my way! She's a child Lib, our child, our baby.' Dad sat down at the kitchen table head in his hands and I knew the anger and fear had dissolved into tears.

'No, you wouldn't want to upset Margaret, would you?' I heard Mam mutter under her breath. 'Alf, Sam has just told me. Well, he thinks they've been in a relationship for sometime.' Mam spoke louder knowing Dad hadn't heard her first remark, she put an arm round his shoulders.

Dad raised his head and stared at me through tear blurred eyes. The coldness in them made me shudder. 'You knew!' He said, his voice low as if he was struggling to keep control. 'You knew!'

In bewilderment I nodded, I knew then I was in for it.

Mam kept a firm arm round Dad's shoulders stopping him from rising.

'How could you know? Why in God's name didn't you say anything? We...I could have put a stop to this. You stupid, stupid idiot Sam. What were you thinking? You must have known no good would come out of this. Oh God Lib, I should never, never have let you persuade me to allow her even to go anywhere near a garage. I assume that's where she met him?'

I nodded, not daring to speak. I wanted to be away from that kitchen, but my feet were rooted to the spot.

'Bloody Lister, obviously takes after his damn Father!' Dad railed his voice rising again in anger. 'I'll swing for them both!'

'Now please Alf, calm down.' Mam tried to sound calm herself but she was struggling.

'Calm down, don't you think that man has caused me enough trouble in the past without this? I swear Lib, I'll kill him and his lad!' The venom that shone in Dad's eyes left me wondering what the past had to do with this, what had happened?

'Look Alf,' Mam said quietly, 'We don't even know if the Father of Ede's bairn is this Tom Lister. Let's wait till she's home before you do or say anything you'll regret.'

Dad looked defeated and I think he knew she was right, he seemed to relax in the chair and remained seated when Mam removed her arm.

'Now I'd best get on with dinner our Ede'll be starving when she comes home.' Mam tried to sound cheerful. I knew she just wanted something to do.

'I'll go and have a look and ask round again if anyone has seen our Ede.' I said reaching up for my jacket.

Mam nodded. Dad looked about to rise to come with me. He stared through me as Mam told him to stay put. 'Let our Sam go.' She told him. 'The girls might tell him something whereas they won't you.'

I was glad to escape from Dad's accusing eyes. Yes it was perhaps all my fault. I should have told them about Ede's affair. Put a stop to it myself even. Pulled Tom Lister to task about it long before now. Surely he could see it was a crush our Ede had on him. Surely he could see that.

He'd used her. Some blokes do that. No doubt he'd brag about his conquest to his mates in the pub. They'd all be lining up for a go. The thought turned my stomach. How could my own sex be like that regarding women, girls. I knew then I would never ever use anyone like that.

Joe confided in me once he'd been to Chapletown

and found a prostitute. She'd taught him all he needed to know about sex. He said I should go. I was appalled by the very idea of it and told him so. He called me names and suggested I was a homosexual. We didn't speak for weeks after that little confrontation.

If he knew how I had felt about Mrs Rowntree and now about Phyllis Lister he would forget that idea. But no way could I, or would I, tell him about either of them.

I trawled my way round Ede's friends again and still no sign. I stood on the corner at the bottom of our street, racking my brains. Phyllis had said countryside, had she gone to the nursery where I worked? That was the only bit of countryside I knew. I went home and got my bike out. Slowly cycling towards my work, peering up this street and the next for a girl, any girl with a pony tail, anyone who looked like Ede.

There was no sign of her anywhere round the nursery and being Sunday it was locked up. A high fence surrounded the place, so I knew no one could get in or out. This made me feel content, knowing no one could get in and damage my precious plants. I cycled home hoping and praying she would be there when I got back.

Mam was sitting at the kitchen table when I got back, I could see pans of vegetables on the kitchen side and smell something cooking in the oven. She'd been busy.

'Dad?' I queried quietly.

'Gone out again Sam,' she shook her head when I

asked where. 'I don't know Sam, he could be anywhere. I just hope he hasn't gone to the Listers. But then if Margaret is there he won't start anything. Or at least I don't think he will, he's no match for the Lister lads is he?'

'Do you want me to go and see Mam?' I wanted to ask questions but they remained unsaid. I asked myself instead who's Margaret? She wasn't one of the Lister girls, but seemingly whoever she was she had influence over Dad? Was it Mrs Lister?

Mam nodded, 'Yes please Sam, go and see if you can find him?'

I was loathe to leave her. 'You will wait here Mam, won't you?'

'Yes Sam, I'll stay here, Ede could be home anytime.'

'Yes Mam and someone ought to be here.'

Ten minutes later I was knocking for a third time on the flaking paint. Sadie opened it, her hair hanging down partially covering her face. 'Yes?' She asked, annoyance in her voice. Had I woken her up? I apologised and asked if she had seen Ede or my Dad.

'No I haven't, oh God isn't she back yet?' Sadie pushed the hair back out of her eyes.

'Sadie think, do you know where she might be? Anything?' I clutched at straws, surely someone must know something. 'Sadie, Tom where is he?'

'Still out, look Sam we are as worried as you lot are. Tom said she'd run off after telling him about the baby. He blames himself...'

'So he bloody well should!' I snapped. 'She's a child!'

'Sam calm down, getting angry won't solve anything. What's done is done. Tom feels bad enough. He loves her you know, he really does. What's more Ede loves him too.'

'Bah! She's fifteen, doesn't know what love is.' I echoed my Dad's words.

'I wouldn't be so sure about that Sam.'

I held my tongue, thinking I wasn't much older when I fell for Mrs Rowntree.

'Tom did say something about a barn over Kirkstall way. He was going to look there. Seems that's where, well...' Her voice trailed off in embarrassment.

'Lets hope he finds her before something happens to her or she does something silly then.' I looked down avoiding her eyes, my head whirling at these thoughts.

'Sam she...she wouldn't, would she?' Sadie clutched her throat.

'I don't know Sadie.' I looked up and saw her horrified expression. 'I just don't know my sister anymore.' I turned to go muttering my thanks.

'Sam,' she called, 'I'll get changed and go out again myself. 'She'll be okay I promise you that.'

How could she promise that. I nodded and walked slowly down the street. Praying Tom Lister would find her. Should I go myself to Kirkstall? I had no idea where this barn was. Half of me was afraid to go and perhaps find Ede...

A tear rolled down my cheek and I brushed it away.

I knew Ede could be so rash and hot headed, if she

thought the world was against her she might do something stupid. I couldn't bring myself to even think the words in my head. Why did she have to be so headstrong and foolish? Why couldn't she be like normal girls, wanting a normal life, interested in pop music and makeup at her age?

I returned home to find Mam sobbing in Ike's arms. She looked up when I walked in. 'Any sign Sam?'

'No Mam not either of them, Sadie said Tom had mentioned a barn out Kirkstall way.' I told them.

'Tom...Tom Lister?' Ike pushed Mam away and stared at me. It was obvious Mam hadn't told him. 'Just what has Tom Lister got to do with any of this?' Ike looked from Mam to me.

I opened my mouth to speak but Mam jumped in.

'Didn't she go there with them fishing or something Sam?' Her guarded look told me Dad knowing about Tom was bad enough, but Ike knowing would be worse.

'With Tom Lister!' Ike barked.

'No with a crowd of them I don't know if he was among them...' Mam's voice trailed off knowing she had just made the situation worse. She stood between Ike and the door. 'Look you're Dad'll be back soon lets just wait and see if he's found her.'

Hazel Stevens

Part Four

Hazel Stevens

1 - Scared

I woke with a start and for a moment couldn't fathom where on earth I was. Realisation soon hit me. I stared round the empty barn, sleep had made me cold so I sat up and hugged my knees in a vain attempt to get warm. Tears filled my eyes. Why couldn't my family understand? Be happy for me. I guess Alice had been right all along. Tom didn't want me, not seriously. His face told me that when I broke the news of my pregnancy. I couldn't stop the tears coming again and sobbed loudly. I felt so very alone, for the first time in my short life there was no one I could turn to. Alice had betrayed my secret and told Ike. It seemed Mam agreed with Dad and Ike that getting rid of it was the best way forward. Not for me though. I wanted this baby, Tom's baby. But I also wanted Tom too.

I must have cried myself back to sleep for when I next stirred, faint shafts of sunlight pierced the walls. Just quite how long I'd been there asleep I had no idea. My stomach rumbled it's hunger.

I got myself up and went cautiously outside. A few sheep scattered from the door as I opened it. They stopped a short way off and stared at me inquisitively. I hastened to the stream, cupped my hands and drank deeply, before splashing water over my face. 'No good feeling sorry for yourself Ede Wagstaff.' I told myself firmly.

However returning to the barn I saw the foolishness of my actions. There I was in a barn, in the middle of nowhere, well almost. No money. No food and not even a coat. How stupid was I?

The usual morning sickness wasn't bothering me that morning. Perhaps I was getting over it. I knew it was a sign of pregnancy in the early weeks, but how long it went on for I had no idea. At times it was so bad, I felt ill all day. But that morning I felt fine. If it wasn't for the deep despair hanging over me.

I lay back down and stared into the rafters. I could see dark shapes hanging close together.

Bats, they had been the creatures flying out of the barn at dusk. I watched for some movement but they remained quite still. A scurrying came to my ears and I turned round to see a mouse staring at me from the top of a stone jutting out of the wall.

Mice have never really scared me. I remembered them coming into our house once, just after they had pulled down an empty factory in the next street to ours. Everyone in our street was infested. Dad set traps as did everyone else, cats were seen carrying dead bodies of mice down the alley.

Soon, thanks to traps and cats, the houses were mice free.

I felt tears in my eyes as I thought about home. Could I go back? No. I told myself there was no way. If Dad didn't kill me then Ike certainly would. I wondered if Sam had told them about Tom. Oh God please, no. He may not want me, but I didn't want him hurt by Dad or Ike. If Sam said anything about Tom then they would guess he was the Father. What had I done, he could go to prison like Alice said. I was too young. I realised that now. But I loved Tom with all my heart and our love making felt right, at least to me. 'Tom, oh Tom.' I moaned. 'Everything was going to be perfect, our own garage and family.' I sobbed into the hay and dozed again.

'Ede, Ede.'

I must have been dreaming, someone was calling my name, I rubbed my eyes and shrank back into the hay as someone pulled open the door. With the bright sunlight behind the figure, I couldn't make out who it was.

'What...do you want?' I stammered.

'Ede, oh my Ede.' Tom said gently, coming over and taking me in his arms. 'I've been looking for you all night. I had no idea you might come here.'

Tom was here, his arms round me. This wasn't happening. I was dreaming. Wasn't I?

'Tom?' I managed to speak.

'I'm here my love.'

He called me his love, I must be dreaming. I shook myself and he wrapped me tighter in his arms. 'Tom, the...the baby.'

'Oh Ede,' he said.

Here it comes, the brush off, he too was going to tell me to get rid of it.

'My Ede. I've found you, everyone has been looking.'

'You don't want me or the baby, do you?' I said accusingly, after all it was his fault I had run away.

'Yes, I do want you...both. I was, well just so surprised and okay I'll admit shocked. But I do want you both if that's what you want. You're so young. I thought if you get to Wharton you'll forget all about me.'

'No! Tom no.' I cried. 'I love you, I really do love you.'

'And I love you too, both of you,' he whispered into my hair. He held me for a long time, before holding me away. 'Are you sure you want this baby Ede? Cos we could well you know. I...I have some money.'

'No! Please don't tell me or even ask me to consider that, it's our baby Tom.'

'Well if you are completely sure, I'm thrilled.' He grinned, kissing my face and finally finding my lips. 'But you're so young,' he added thoughtfully.

'Old enough to know I want to be with you and have our baby Tom. What shall we call him or her.' I said impulsively.

'Steady on Ede, first we have to get you home and face your Mam and Dad.'

'No Tom, can't we just leave right now, go somewhere far away, you could get a job in any garage...I'm not going home...Dad will...will kill us both.'

'Don't exaggerate Ede, you must go back and let them know you're at least safe. If your Dad throws you out, which he might, but he won't kill you. If he does throw you out then you can live at ours till we get sorted and find somewhere of our own.'

I stared at him. I knew he was right, Mam would be worried. Perhaps if I went home she might be there on her own. I could ask her if I could get a few things and leave. Dad and Ike needn't know I'd been. Mam could tell them I rang up or something.

Tom stood up and held out his hand, 'Come on Ede, time to face the music.'

'OK.' I said reluctantly. Taking his hand, he pulled me to my feet. I went on to tell him about the creatures during the night in the barn. I told him how I'd heard funny noises outside and how scared I'd been.

He laughed, tucked his arm round me and told me it would be mice, and probably a badger or something, even a rabbit.

'Rabbits don't grunt.' I snapped.

'OK let's settle on a badger then,' he laughed again and keeping a firm hold of my hand led me out into the sunshine.

'I'm starving Tom.' I said as we approached the road. Tom had come in the van from the garage.

'Right food and then home okay?' He spoke so firmly. I just nodded.

I knew he was right, I had to go home and face whatever music was coming to me. If Tom was by my side I would be okay. He was tall and strong. Dad wouldn't start on him and I was sure he could beat Ike. But did I want them fighting? No, not at all. I told Tom my fears.

'Look one step at a time, lets just see what they say,' he wrapped his arms round me again.

'Once they know I'm going to stand by you I'm sure

they will come round to the idea of us getting married.'

'What what did you say Tom? M...married?'

He nodded and fell down onto one knee, I looked down on him tears filling my eyes again as he said the words I longed to hear. 'Will you marry me?'

2 - Celebration and Confrontation

Tom bought me a shandy at the pub we stopped at to eat. I drank thirstily from the glass. 'Steady on lass, you'll get tiddly and really alchohol is no good for the bairn is it?'

I guiltily placed the glass on the table, 'One won't do it any harm will it?' I felt anxious and then relieved as Tom shook his head and told me we were celebrating our engagement.

I stared down at the third finger on my left hand and grinned. Tom had twisted and woven a ring, an engagement ring, out of grass. He placed it on my finger and repeated his question. 'Well Ede, will you marry me?'

I nodded tears filling my eyes and rolling down my cheeks. 'Yes, oh yes please Tom.'

The tears threatened again now. 'Hey softy this should be a happy meal.' Tom declared. He was right of course, and I was happy, I told him, so happy that I felt my heart would burst and I just wanted to cry. He laughed at me and took my hand, kissing it quickly before letting go as the waitress brought us steak and chips. I'd never had steak like that before and wasn't sure if I'd like it. It tasted so much better than roast beef and I was ravenous, I finished long before Tom. I looked at the menu to see if the pub did puddings. Apple pie and custard, just the job. I wanted to stay there forever just the two of us like an ordinary, engaged couple. Tom soon broke my dream.

'Time to go home Ede.'

I shook my head. 'Do we have to?' I wailed.

'Now look Ede, we have been through all this and yes, I want you to make things right with your Mam and Dad. I'll be there beside you and I will tell your Dad I love you and we shall be married. OK?!'

I nodded and followed him out to the van, our celebrations coming to an abrupt end.

Tom drove the van back to the garage and parked it outside. I was just getting out as Sam came round the corner on his bike. 'Ede,' he shouted at me.

For several minutes Sam ranted and raved at me, questions flying thick and fast, where had I been? What was I doing? Didn't I know how upset they'd all been? He wouldn't allow me to elope either.

I stared at him. Oh yes, I wanted to elope with Tom. Tom wouldn't hear of it, he wanted things to be right.

Sam grabbed my arm, 'Home! Now! Dad and Ike are looking for you too, we've been up half the night. Mam nearly got lost...' his voice trailed off.

I pulled away shaking my head, 'Tom is coming too. Mam...is Mam alright Sam?' I was scared something might have happened to her.

Sam nodded, 'Yes, she's okay but wants you home.'

'I'm not coming without Tom.' I repeated.

'No way Ede, Dad'll kill him, no way will Dad let a Lister over our doorstep,' he stared angrily at Tom.

'Well I'm not coming home then.' I said defiantly.

'You bloody well are and now.' Sam grabbed my arm again and pulled me away from Tom.

'No.' I screamed, looking beseechingly back at Tom. I pulled out of Sam's grip and ran back to him.

I told Sam Tom and I were engaged and I wasn't going home without him.

Sam stared at us both. 'You really think this is a good idea?' He snapped.

Tom and I nodded. He took my hand firmly in his and we followed Sam up the back alley. I hesitated at the back gate. Sam glared and strode up to the back door. I pushed Tom ahead of me but he put his arm through mine and pulled me round beside him.

'Together.' Tom whispered as we followed Sam up to the back door. Making sure we were coming Sam opened it and stood to one side allowing us to go in first.

'She's here.' He called.

Mam ran and flung her arms round me saying my name over and over again, throughthe tears in her voice.

I clutched her too and muttered, 'I'm sorry Mam, but I want my baby and Tom and I are engaged. Where's Dad and Ike, are they here?' I added nervously.

Mam shook her head and looked at Tom. 'You want to marry my girl?'

Tom nodded and told Mam how we'd both been stupid and he was so sorry, but that he did love me, how he had a good job and could look after me and the baby. Yes, we would get married as soon as we could if Dad, or Mr Wagstaff as Tom called him, would give his permission.

'She's not sixteen.' Mam whispered.

'I know and we can wait till she is, baby won't be showing much by then.' Tom told her.

How did he know I wouldn't be showing much? I so wanted to ask and would do later. Then I remembered he was the oldest and would know how his Mam had been when she had the rest of the Lister children.

'Your Dad will never allow this Ede. You should go Tom before him and Ike get back.'

Mam sat down at the table shaking her head.

'No, Mam. Tom stays! If he goes I go!' I felt Tom squeeze my hand, unsure if it was in agreement with my demand or not.

'Be prepared for the worst, both of you.' Mam sighed, getting up she reached for the kettle.

'Sam have a ride round will you, see if you can find them and tell them Ede's home.'

Sam nodded and left, Mam indicated we should both sit down and I could see how nervous Tom was, he sat at the table twisting his hands together. I sat biting my lip and again started telling Mam how sorry I was. How it was all my fault and I wanted Tom and his baby.

Mam just nodded and placed cups of tea in front of us. Again warning us to be prepared as Dad was not happy. I gasped when she said Dad and Ike knew about Tom and me. I half rose from the table.

Tom placed a hand on my arm. 'Together.' He whispered again. I looked at his lovely face and could see the love shining from his brown eyes. I knew I'd be alright with Tom, I just hoped Dad could see that too.

Mam smiled happily at me, she had seen the look that had passed between Tom and me. I swear she knew, oh yes she definitely knew, how much we loved each other. My heart lightened, she'd persuade Dad to give his permission. I reached over and grabbed her hand, squeezing it tightly, giving her my silent thanks, before letting go abruptly as we heard the back gate slam open and shut.

Dad and Ike pushed through the back door together, their mouths fell open as they saw Tom sitting at the kitchen table.

'What the hell is going on here?' Snarled Ike, getting in first, he raised his fist. Sam grabbed Ike's arm and held on for grim death as Ike tried to shake him off. The two of them clattered back down the steps into the yard.

Mam screamed and ran after them. 'Stop it,' she cried 'Stop it. Now.'

Ike and Sam were obviously fighting, I looked at Tom, but Dad stepped in and yelled at them to stop. His raised voice stilled their flailing fists, both of them hung their heads.

'Sorry Dad,' they muttered.

'I still want to get my hands on him.' growled Ike.

'Nobody is laying any more hands on anyone!' Mam stood with her arms folded on the back door step.

Ike made to push past her, she grabbed his shoulder and pushed him back into the yard. 'No one! Do you hear me?! Ede is home and safe and what's more it was Tom who found her.'

I could see round her Dad's face growing redder and redder. I'd never seen him so angry and for a moment I thought he was going to start on Mam and shove her out of the way. Ike may not have got to Tom but Dad was certainly going to try his best. Mam stood firm.

'Calm down you three, I know you're angry and they know they have done wrong. But it's as much Ede's fault as it is Tom's,' she said. Boldly defying anyone to argue.

'She's a child.' Dad squeaked through gritted teeth. 'I'll get the law!' Turning to retreat out the back gate.

'No, Dad please no.' I cried over Mam's shoulder.

'No Alf, no police. We do not want this all over the papers, do we?' Mam added in a low voice.

I could see Dad hesitating.

'Alf please come in and listen to what they have to say. Please. You as well Sam and Ike, now!'

The three men of my family came shuffling into the kitchen. Sam looked relieved. Ike looked angry and Dad looked defeated. We all knew his family pride had got the better of him and there was no way he would want the merest hint of a scandal.

The scuffle in the yard could be played off as sibling rivalry. I wasn't quite sure how they would explain my pregnancy.

Tom stood up and put out his hand across the table

towards Dad, 'Mr Wagstaff, first I am sorry Ede went missing, that was my fault. I'm here to make amends.'

Dad ignored him.

'I've fallen in love with your daughter and I would like your permission, as soon as she is old enough, to marry Ede.' Tom continued. 'I want to be a proper Father to my child.'

I couldn't stop grinning at this wonderful speech. It meant the world to me. Surely Dad would agree.

'Pah! What would you know about being a proper Father?' Dad sneered. 'You know how to make 'em that's obvious, but how would you begin to know what being a decent Father is with that bastard you call Father.'

'Alf please.' Mam held him back as Dad tried to move round the table to Tom.

'Tom you'd better go, let us sort this out ourselves now, you've had your say. We'll talk it over and see what's what.'

'No Mam.' I screamed, 'Tom please don't leave. They'll make me get rid of it, please, its not what we planned. I love you. I'm coming with you. I told you Mam, if Tom goes I go!'

'You'll stay here girl!' Dad yelled at me. 'Love, love you're way too young to know what love is. You will do as I say, do you hear! Yes, getting rid of it is the best option.'

Tom moved round the table and squared up to Dad. 'This is my child Mr Wagstaff and it will only be got rid of if that's what Ede decides. I can't make myself any clearer on that. Only to repeat I love your daughter and if she'll have me I want to marry her and look after them both.'

'Oh yes, Tom yes.' I squealed with delight. 'I am keeping this baby Dad.'

'Mmmph!' Dad grunted, his face still red with anger.

'Tom please let us talk to Ede.' Mam pushed Dad to one side so Tom could leave. 'Ike move now,' she added glaring at her eldest son.

I could see Ike was itching to thump Tom and begged Tom to stay.

'Your Mam's right Ede this is no good, everyone needs to calm down. I'll go and come back later when I hope to be able to talk to you again Mr and Mrs Wagstaff. I am serious about Ede!'

'He is Dad.' I pleaded, 'Look we're engaged.' I thrust my left hand with its shrivelled band of grass on my finger.

Dad shrugged and strode off into the living room, slamming the door behind him.

Ike made a move towards Tom.

'Ike please.' I begged.

Ike turned to look at me, I could see his eyes soften as he no doubt saw my distraught face. He turned back to Tom and muttered under his breath. 'Don't think you've got away with this Lister.'

'Ike.' Mam said firmly.

Tom left me sitting at the kitchen table. I knew for now I had no alternative but to stay and try to make them see how much I cared for Tom, and he for me. 'I love you,' I mouthed. Tom smiled and was gone.

I felt secure in the knowledge that I didn't think anyone would hurt me, well not physically.

Ike got mad at times but had never laid a finger on me, Dad had always been strict about that. It was terrifying when Dad slapped me and now to see him nearly hit Mam made me feel worse. Tom, however was different, Ike would flatten him for sure if he got chance. Mam firmly laid the law down to Ike and Sam. Telling them both to leave Tom alone, that no good would come having a go at him and perhaps getting into trouble with the police themselves. 'You've Alice and the children to think of Ike.'

My big brother looked down at his shoes, he too looked defeated.

'Please Ike, I love Tom, please don't hurt him.' I whispered.

'Did he force you Ede?' Ike asked quietly.

I shook my head.

'You're sure cos if he did I will kill him!' He affirmed viciously.

'No Ike, I made love with Tom, he didn't force me. I wanted him. He didn't want to, so I thought he didn't love me. It was just so...' I broke off on the edge of tears.

'Mmmph...!' Growled Ike sounding just like Dad. 'I'm back home then. Alice said she'd got names of well you know, if...if.'

'No Ike, this is my baby, mine and Tom's. I am not going to get rid! If you try to make me, any of you, then

I shall run away again. I promise you that.' I could feel the anger rising at the back of my throat, 'Mam, tell him please.'

'You heard her Ike, now please go and stay away from Tom Lister.' Mam shooed him out the door and rather begrudgingly, it seemed, Ike nodded and left.

I just prayed Ike would go home and not after Tom.

'Mam, I'm not getting rid of it.' I ran to her sobbing in her arms.

'No Ede, no one is going to make you do that if you really don't want to. I will see to that!'

Sam discreetly moved quietly away and I was so relieved Mam was on my side, she would make Dad see. Everything was going to be alright and if it wasn't then I wouldn't stay, I told Mam.

'No one is going anywhere lass, for now you're home is here with us,' she said holding me tightly.

3 - Acceptance

I sat back down at the kitchen table, bewildered by it all. I felt lost. Tom wasn't here to support me, would they now try and persaude me to abort my baby?

'It's OK Ede, I think we are all certain you want this baby. I know, or at least hope Tom will support you. But you're so young, what about college? Your life ahead?' Mam sighed and sat down opposite me, she held out her hands.

'This is what I want Mam.' I said taking hold of both her hands.

She nodded, 'Are you hungry?'

I shook my head telling her of the wonderful meal Tom and I had shared only a hour since, yet it felt like ages ago. 'I'd like a bath though Mam.'

'Yes I bet you do, sleeping in an old barn,' she laughed. 'Off you go then, I'll talk to your Dad. But I can't make any promises Ede. You know how he feels about the Listers.'

'Mam, you will persuade him, won't you? He'll see when Tom comes back, he will see how much Tom does love me and I love him Mam honest I do. He'll see Tom is not like his Father. I promise you that Mam he really isn't!'

Mam nodded and dropped my hands as she shooed me away, she swallowed back the tears and I heard her murmer. 'My grown up girl.'

I lay in the bath for a long time, dozing for most of it, waking up only when the water turned cold. I topped the bath up with hot until, when, there was no more left and I had to get out. I felt better and refreshed. I was glad it wasn't Saturday night and Ike was still at home, waiting to get ready to go out. He'd go mad if there was no hot water. I'd heard him ranting at our Sam many times over it.

I rubbed my hair as dry as I could and in my room I put it in a long plait. I thought plaiting it made me look older than in just a pony tail. I applied a light dusting of face powder and some very pale lipstick. Didn't want to aggravate Dad further, he hated girls wearing lots of make up. I had born the brunt of that returning home once from Sadie's. She had done a makeover on me. I had thick black eye-liner above and below my eyes. Really dark red lipstick. All the fashion, Sadie told me, as she back combed my hair so it stood up over my head and the rest hung down round my face. I thought I looked so grown up and couldn't wait to get home to show off my new look.

Dad went beserk and marched me upstairs himself to wash 'that muck' off my face. It took me ages and I still had dark shadows round my eyes. Sadie said I should have used some special make up remover. Of course all I had was soap and water which made it look worse. I promised Dad I wouldn't go that far again with make up.

'You won't go anywhere with it our Ede,' he said firmly. 'You have a nice face, what do you want to ruin it with that muck for, besides you're not old enough to wear make up.'

I wanted to yell at him I was old enough but the look on his face told me to keep my mouth shut. I only wore the merest hint after that and I'm not sure if he noticed, perhaps Mam had told him not to comment, as he never did.

Tea was a silent meal, even Sam said nothing, he usually prattled on about his plants. After tea he announced he was going round to Joe's for the evening.

Mam nodded and reminded him it was Sunday, not to be late, as work tomorrow. She also told him to take a coat as it might rain or be cold when he came home.

I smiled, I guessed once a Mam always a Mam. Would I be like that with my child? I realised then I would have to keep reminding myself otherwise I would be just like my parents.

Well Mam was okay, but Dad had such old fashioned ideas.

I helped with the washing up, Dad took himself off into the living room. Sometimes on Sundays we'd use the front sitting room, but since Ike moved out of there we'd hardly used it at all. Mam's birthday that's all, when Great Aunt Eliza came over from Harrogate. I hadn't seen her for sometime and gasped when I saw how old she looked. Yet still so tall, smart and sprightly with all her wits about her. She was in her nineties then.

I ran to the back door when I heard the quiet knock.

Tom, I threw myself into his arms, kissing him on his face, his lips, he smelt wonderful. I could see he'd really made an effort as he wore a suit with a shirt and tie. He'd shaved and the wonderful smell was the aftershave I'd bought him for Easter. Tom didn't eat chocolate, didn't like it he told me. So instead of an egg I got him the aftershave. He'd got me a huge Easter chocolate bunny. I ate it all at one go and ended up feeling quite sick afterwards. Tom told me it served me right.

'Tom, come in come in.' I pulled him over the doorstep into the kitchen.

'Hello lad,' Mam said kindly, 'Can I get you a drink, tea or something?'

'No thanks Mrs Wagstaff. I'd like to talk calmly to you and your husband about Ede. If I may that is.' Tom smiled.

Mam nodded and led us into the living room. Dad put down his paper and stared at me. Tom instinctively put a protective arm round my shoulders.

'I meant what I said this afternoon Mr Wagstaff, I love and admire your Ede. I want to marry her with your permission on her sixteenth birthday. I'm sure we can arrange it for then.' Tom said quietly, his arm tightening round my shoulders as he spoke. 'Please Mr Wagstaff, you're Ede is an amazing young woman. Her mechanical knowledge and skills are second to none.'

'We aren't here to discuss my daughter's skills.' Dad bristled as he interrupted Tom. 'We are here to discuss why I shouldn't go to the police and report you.'

'Alf.' Mam gasped. 'We've talked about this earlier

and you promised.'

'Well.' Dad's voice was low and quite menacing. 'Just give me one good reason why I shouldn't Lister!'

'Dad please,' my tears threatened. Keep calm Ede I told myself. 'Dad please listen to what we have to say.'

'Yes Alf, at least we should hear them out.' Mam agreed.

Dad looked from one to the other of us and muttered, 'Looks like I've no choice! OK lad, tell me what these grand plans are that you both seem to think you have!'

Tom opened his mouth to speak, but I jumped in impatiently and told Dad we planned to get married, get our own garage. Tom and I could work together and bring up our baby.

'I asked him!' Dad growled.

'Well s...sir. I would like to marry Ede as soon as we are allowed to. I have a little money put by, maybe enough for a deposit on a small garage. It would be good if we could find one with a flat above, though I know this is not always possible. Ede could go to night school, if she wants to, learn book keeping. Just like she was going to do at Wharton...' Tom trailed off.

'Well you certainly think you've got it all nicely planned out haven't you!' Dad snarled sarcastically. 'How do I know you're not going to end up like your old man? Letting his poor wife work all hours while he sits on his backside!'

'It seems obvious to me you despise my Father Mr Wagstaff, as I and the rest of my family do. Many times we have tried to get my Mother to stop working so hard, to even leave him. But to no avail. She loves him Mr Wagstaff, what more can I say?'

'Bah, she doesn't even know what love really is.' Dad replied. 'Nor does our Ede, she's a child. What will you do when she gets fed up of playing at being a wife and mother? No Ede, that is a possibility,' he held up his hands to silence my protest.

I tried my best to deny that anything like that would happen and was miffed Dad stopped me. When he'd finished I just murmered. 'I won't.'

'Ede's Dad and I had a long talk this afternoon.' Mam said slowly, directing her attention to Tom.

I wasn't prepared for what she had to say next, I closed my eyes, heart in my mouth, waiting for their decision. I held onto Tom and could feel myself shaking. He too was trembling a little.

'Yes, what did you decide?' Tom asked cautiously.

'Well...' Mam seemed to be struggling for the right words.

Here it comes, here it comes. They want me to get rid. I held my breath. I wanted to be anywhere but in that room. I would leave with Tom that minute. I pulled his hand, Tom stood upright waiting to hear what she had to say.

'Well, it's obvious to see you really do care for Ede.' Mam began.

Tom nodded furiously, 'Oh I do.'

'Well,' Mam began again. 'We think the best course of action is for Ede to finish school. No one need know about her pregnancy. It's very early days. I will take Ede to a doctor in a week or two to make sure she really is pregnant.'

I opened my mouth, but Mam raised her hand.

'Ede if you are, then you and Tom have our permission to get married on your sixteenth birthday.'

'Oh Mam.' I cried throwing myself into her arms. 'Thank you, thank you, thank you.'

'Your Dad agreed too,' she said.

'Dad thank you.' I went towards him but he waved me away. 'Tom isn't that wonderful?' I cried rushing back to Tom's side.

Tom was shaking Mam's hand and thanking her enthusiastically. He turned to Dad and held out his hand. 'Thank you sir you will not regret this. I will look after Ede and our baby I promise you that.'

Dad ignored Tom's outstretched hand. 'You'd better,' he said, picking up his newspaper.

I was too happy to take any offence at this. I noticed Tom frown. Later when I was seeing Tom out, he told me he thought that my Dad would be hoping I wasn't pregnant. So I wouldn't have to get married.

'Tom.' I said uncertainly, 'But would you still want to marry me?'

'Of course you daft girl,' he said, picking me up and swinging me round in our yard. 'Now come on with me, I think this is a good time to make sure you are pregnant,' he whispered, taking my hand.

'Oh Tom! Let's do just that!' I giggled.

Hazel Stevens

Part Five

Hazel Stevens

1 - The Wedding

Well I couldn't believe my ears, Dad had actually agreed to Ede marrying Tom Lister! Maybe there could be a chance for me and Phyllis. 'Who knows or dares to dream.' sprang to my mind.

Over the next few weeks Ede seemed to mature before our eyes. Most days, after school, she would go to the garage and would come home covered in oil and grease. Mam would tut and tell her, she was sure it wouldn't do the baby any good.

I kept my thoughts to myself, if Ede had been my daughter, there'd be no wedding, at just sixteen. She well, she...! Really I didn't know what I'd do in that situation and I hoped if I ever had daughters I never would be.

Arrangements had begun in earnest for the forthcoming ceremony and it was here the arguments began. Tom and Ede told us they wanted a quiet registry office do and a few drinks afterwards.

Mam was horrified, Ede was her only daughter and she wanted the best for her. It wasn't until Dad put his foot down and told the young couple firmly, if they were to be married, it had to be done properly in church or not at all.

Ede complained bitterly and said it would be a mockery, her being pregnant and all. Dad stood firm and said he didn't want everyone to think it was a rush gun point do in some office.

So a church wedding was organised and I don't think anyone mentioned Ede's condition to the vicar. He had been very surprised that my Dad had given his permission for the ceremony. He had lectured Tom and Ede several times, by all accounts, trying to persuade them they were too young, well Ede certainly was.

So it went on and on, I tell you, I was glad to escape to work, to my room and stick my head in my gardening magazines and books.

Ede finished school and came home on her last day in tears. She told us the teachers had all been so lovely and wished them all well, especially herself, Lucy and Amy Brigshaw who were going to Wharton. Ede said she felt so guilty and wanted to tell them the truth.

Dad had warned Ede, he would not tolerate any of us talking about the baby or, for the moment, the wedding. I think he was still coming to terms with the whole idea.

Ede had in fact told Lucy she wouldn't be going to Wharton, at least not full time and it seemed Lucy had agreed to be Ede's bridesmaid. Gradually other friends and neighbours got to know about the forthcoming nuptials. From overhearing Mam and Dad, quite a few people had been appalled at the idea with Ede being so young and even a couple of neighbours had blatantly asked our Mam straight out if she, Ede, was pregnant? Mam arrived home from the shops that particular day in a right flap. She told us she had denied it, but knew it would soon be common knowledge.

At one point I cautiously asked if Ede and Tom

would live with us after the wedding.

'Indeed they won't.' Dad told us firmly.

Mum sadly agreed it wouldn't be a good idea and for now they would be living at the Lister's or so she assumed. However I think both Mam and Dad were both a lot happier when Ede came home and told us Tom had found them a flat near the garage and he was moving into it the following week.

'He wants to get it ready for us and the baby, before the wedding.' Ede enthused. 'Mam I could perhaps, well perhaps move in too?'

'You certainly will not girl!' Dad roared. 'You will stay here until after, well after the wed... after its legal.'

I knew then Dad was still struggling with the idea, I could not be sure if it was because Ede had got herself into trouble and had to get married so young, or was it because the groom was a Lister? I just hoped it would be the first, my mind often being on Phyllis. I met her, accidentally you understand, and just being able to spend a few moments with her was a treat in itself. I couldn't take it any further. One Lister in the family was quite enough for Mam and Dad to cope with.

The day finally arrived and we all waited patiently for Ede to come downstairs in her dress. I'd heard her earlier pleading to Mam that she would look like a meringue in her dress, but when she came into the living room we all gasped.

'See I told you I looked silly Mam.' Ede cried turning to our Mam.

'No no its just...' We all said at once.

Dad stood up and said in a choked voice. 'You look stunning my girl.'

We all nodded and added our praise, she did indeed look beautiful and I vowed to tell her myself properly later.

Ede turned to Ike 'Do you really think so?'

He nodded and I could see he was lost in his own thoughts. Alice had tears in her eyes, as did our Mam and Dad, I wasn't far off.

'Now get to the church all of you.' Dad ordered. 'I want some time with my daughter before the car arrives.

Ede looked panic stricken, 'You...you're not going to try and change my mind Dad, are you?'

'No lass, you've made your decision and from what I've seen of Tom over these last weeks well he thinks a lot of you as you do him.'

We left them with Ede throwing her arms round Dad's neck, and Dad returned her embrace.

Mam led Ike's family outside and we made our way down the road, with her clutching onto Shirley for grim death as the little girl tried to walk all over. Mam was worried she'd fall and ruin her bridesmaid dress. Alice looked bonny in her dress and the two of them were a picture going down the aisle, with Lucy behind following Ede and my Dad.

Tom and his friend Maurice stood up at the front, looking very smart in matching suits and ties. They wore those thin ties and winkle pickers, which looked a decade out of date. But then these chaps had grown up in that era. So it had obviously stuck.

I pulled at my tie, eager for it to be off. Mam slapped my hand away gently. I looked over and saw Phyllis grinning at me. I knew my face turned red in embarrassment, I mean a man of my age being remonstrated by his Mother!

Phyllis Lister looked lovely, her long blonde hair loose, soft and shiny. The blue in her dress matched her eyes. I felt Ike give me a nudge. He saw I couldn't take my eyes off the girl and suddenly I was aware the service was about to start.

Margaret and Fred Lister looked happy, Fred looked almost smug and I saw Margaret wipe a tear from her eye.

Thankfully it was finally over and the photos had been taken. We were finally installed in the Grey Horse pub and I could take my tie off at last. My jacket came off too. It was a warm day and most of the men had done the same.

There was a buffet meal and the Lister lads were first there, with their Father, to help themselves.

'I hope they leave some for the rest of us.' Dad growled quietly eyeing their full plates.

'Now Alf don't spoil it.' Mam whispered.

Dad turned to her and said lowly that only Mam and I heard. 'I hope you aren't expecting me to be civil to that man, are you?'

'Maybe Alf, just for today please.' Mam begged him.

Dad stood up and announced he was going to get

something to eat while there was still something left. I turned to Mam and saw tears once more in her eyes.

'Mam what is it?' I asked as gently as I could.

'Oh Sam,' she began. 'Nothing really just me being silly, and the day. Ede looks so happy, doesn't she?'

I glanced across at my sister with her arm linked in her husband's, she was talking animatedly to her Mother in Law and Sadie. Mam gasped when we saw Sadie touch Ede's extended stomach, which had not really been hidden under the dress.

I'd heard several comments from people in the church about Ede's condition and how they thought we were trying to keep it quiet. Great Aunt Eliza heard too. She turned and asked sarcastically if they had never made a mistake, she'd added something about let him without sin cast the first stone. I guessed the latter was from the bible.

Dad had joined Ede, Tom, Margaret and Sadie. I saw him touch Margaret's arm and he smiled at her. She returned the smile and nodded.

My attention turned back to Mam as she sighed deeply.

'What is it Mam?' I asked again.

'Margaret Lister,' she said.

'But I thought you had got to know her a bit and liked her too?'

'Oh I do and your Dad does too. As you can see.'

I gasped myself as I saw Dad lean over and kiss the woman we were talking about on the cheek.

At that moment Fred Lister strode up and clapped

Dad on the back. The man had obviously had quite a bit to drink. 'Now then Wagstaff.' Fred said too loudly. Conversation ceased and it seemed the whole room was listening, well most of the older guests were. 'Never thought I'd live to see the day when we'd be related.' Fred Lister roared.

I could see Dad struggling to keep calm, his face reddening in anger.

'Alf leave it.' Margaret Lister said, standing between my Dad and her husband.

Dad turned away and retreated back to our table, leaving Fred Lister beaming after him, before clasping Margaret round the waist and murmuring something in her ear.

'Thank you Alf.' Mam said handing Dad his glass of beer.

The day went on. Fred Lister and some of his sons seemed to be really enjoying the drink.

In the huddle on the small dance floor, amidst writhing bodies attempting to do the twist, I found Phyllis and had the chance to hold her in my arms for a few minutes as we swayed to the music. Not easy to the fast beat of Twist and Shout. But we managed and it was heaven.

'Phyllis.' I took my chance. 'Would you like to g... go...out with me?'

'Oh yes,' she breathed, impulsively kissing me on the cheek. I lifted my head and saw Dad staring at us through the crowd.

'Good.' I said, 'We'll arrange something later, right

now I need a word with my Dad okay?'

Phyllis nodded and I made my way across the room. Dad was on his own at our table. Ike, Alice and the kids were jumping about the dance floor. Mam was over talking to Ede and Tom.

'Dad, are you okay?' I asked tentatively.

'Not you as well?' He murmured taking a long drink of beer. 'What is it with these Listers?'

'Dad, Phyllis is different.' I sat down beside him.

'Bah different, how can she be different with that man as her Father?'

'I don't know Dad, but I know she is. She's not a bit brash and loud like Sadie and the others. Tom ain't like that either. You'll like her Dad, I know you will.' I added rather lamely.

'I can see you do!'

'Well yes, I do as a matter of fact, I really do, and what's more Dad I've asked her to go out with me!' I held my breath waiting for him to explode.

He sat back in his chair and grinned instead, 'Takes after her Mother that one, the image of Margaret at her age.'

'You knew Margaret Lister Dad?'

'Yes,' he sighed, leaning towards me. 'Knew her and more than knew her. I was in love Sam, can't have been much older than you. So yes, in lots of ways I can understand how you and...and even our Ede feels.' Dad sat back and I could see sadness in his eyes.

'What happened Dad?'

'Fred bloody Lister is what happened! Stepped in

before I had the chance, swept her off her feet. She said she had fallen in love! I didn't stand a chance, he was so brash!'

'But Mam?' I was worried, I thought he loved Mam, was it all an act? I wanted to ask but didn't need to.

'Well your Mam is a different kettle of fish altogether. When I met her, I realised my feelings for Margaret weren't that deep. I love your Mam Sam, so take that worried look off your face. Love her and always will. Even though she still thinks I have feelings for Margaret. Don't you Lib?'

'Your mouth running away with you Alf is it?' Mam laughed, coming back to our table, she indicated how he'd had rather a lot to drink. She sat herself down beside him and kissed him on the cheek.

'Nope, just explaining love to my lad here,' he pulled her over and kissed her on the lips. 'I know you think I still hold a torch for an old flame,' he added nodding in Margaret's direction. 'But you know as well as I do Lib you are the love of my life and always will be, do you hear!'

It was Mam's face that turned red now, as she pushed him away she laughingly said, 'Well, they say a drunken man always speaks the truth.'

I was so relieved and realised I could go ahead and date Phyllis, who knows where that would lead? Only time would tell.

Today though was Ede's day. Even I felt a lump in my throat when Dad gave a wonderful speech about his daughter saying all he wanted was her happiness. He added with a smile that Tom would have to answer to him if Ede wasn't happy. We all laughed and joined in the toast, raising our glasses to 'Our Ede.'

The End

Hazel Stevens

Index

ISBN : 978-1-911424-08-6
SKU/ID: 9781911424086

ORIGINAL COVER:
Title: OUR EDE
Artist: Fabio Perla
Technique: monochrome pencils on card board
Size: 73 x 51 cm
Year: 2016

Editor: Monica Turoni
Book design by: Wolf

Publishing Company:
Black Wolf Edition & Publishing Ltd.
2 Glebe Place, Burntisland KY3 0ES, Scotland
www.blackwolfedition.com